13 GHOSTLY YARNS

13
GHOSTLY YARNS

Newly Illustrated Revised Edition

Edited by

Elizabeth Hough Sechrist

Illustrations by Albert Michini

MACRAE SMITH COMPANY
Philadelphia

Acknowledgments

The editor wishes to express her appreciation to Charles Scribner's Sons for permission to use "My Grandfather, Hendry Watty" from WANDERING HEATH by Sir Arthur Quiller-Couch; to Harper & Brothers for "A Ghost Story" from SKETCHES NEW AND OLD by Mark Twain, and "The Water Ghost of Harrowby Hall" from WATER GHOSTS AND OTHER STORIES by John Kendrick Bangs; and to Little, Brown & Company for "The Soul of the Great Bell" from SOME CHINESE GHOSTS by Lafcadio Hearn.

To My Husband

*whose wanderings with me through
ghostly lore were an inspiration to
choose the best*

$\succ$ *Preface*

13—*that significant numeral of legendary superstition—is the number of ghost tales chosen for this collection. Primarily the book is intended for the young reader whose tastes lean toward the supernatural: ghosts, spooks, and unfathomable situations of all varieties and any kinds. From my own experience as a storyteller I know that these eager listeners and readers are in the majority, and I know too that ghost stories for them to read are all too scarce. In addition, this collection is intended as a supplementary reader and with that in mind I have endeavored to present here only the best in literature, at the same time excluding the too-horrible, the too-gruesome, the morbid—qualities which are characteristic of ghost collections for the adult reader.*

Humor takes chief place amongst these yarns. In Mark Twain's "Ghost Story" there are haunts to make the blood curdle, and then there is a solution that is as ridiculous as anything this famous humorist has ever concocted. In "Water Ghost" John Kendrick Bangs satirizes the serious ghost tale in his usual subtle, witty style. "The Devil in the Belfry" by Poe is one of the very few humorous stories written by the author of the perfect mystery tale. His description of "Vondervotteimittiss" and the sprightly "devil in the belfry" who appears boldly in broad daylight, causing the clock to strike "thirdeen o'clock!" is an exquisite piece of humor from an ultra-serious mind.

"The Gray Champion" by Hawthorne presents a visionary, or hero ghost. To Lafcadio Hearn we are indebted for the retelling of that beautiful Chinese legend of the heroine Ko-Ngai whose spirit returns with each clap of the great bell in the Ta-chung sz', when Chinese mothers whisper to their children, "Listen! that is Ko-Ngai crying for her shoe!" In "Peter Rugg, the Missing Man" Austin leaves the problem to be solved by the reader; only the ghostly facts are presented. With Marley's Ghost we are all familiar. As for the ghost of Hamlet's father, it would not seem fitting to omit that apparition from this collection. In the story of Hendry Watty, Sir Arthur Quiller-Couch explains away those weird happenings by the fact that Hendry Watty had drunk too much "eggy hot"; while Kipling, in his two stories from India, would have us believe that he really has no faith at all in ghosts!

In a few instances there have been certain words, sentences, and occasionally paragraphs omitted from the original versions of these stories.

And now the thirteen tales are sent forth with the hope that all who read them may derive some pleasure from them and feel the desire to go back to them again and again because they are old friends.

ELIZABETH HOUGH SECHRIST

⤜ Contents

13 GHOSTLY YARNS

A GHOST STORY

by Mark Twain

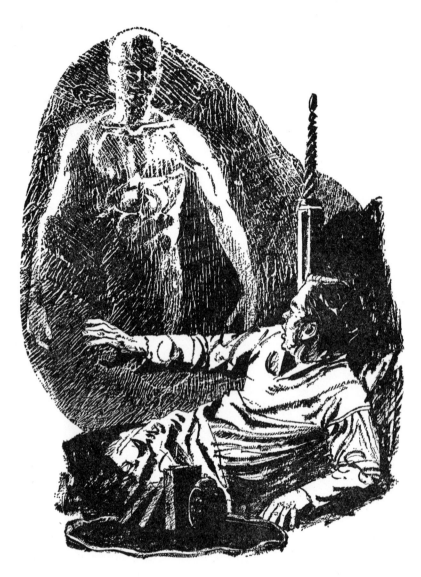

The majestic Cardiff Giant loomed above me!

⤕ *One*

I TOOK a large room, far up Broadway, in a huge old building whose upper stories had been wholly unoccupied for years until I came. The place had long been given up to dust and cobwebs, to solitude and silence. I seemed groping among the tombs and invading the privacy of the dead, that first night I climbed up to my quarters. For the first time in my life a superstitious dread came over me; and as I turned a dark angle of the stairway and an invisible cobweb swung its sleazy woof in my face and clung there, I shuddered as one who had encountered a phantom.

I was glad enough when I reached my room and locked out the mold and darkness. A cheery fire was burning in the grate, and I sat down before it with a comforting sense of relief. For two hours I sat there, thinking of bygone times; recalling old scenes, and summoning half-forgotten faces out of the mists of the past; listening, in fancy, to voices that long ago grew silent for all time, and to once familiar songs that nobody sings now. And as my reverie softened down to a sadder and sadder pathos, the shrieking of the winds outside softened to a wail, the angry beating of the rain against the panes diminished to a tranquil patter, and one by one the noises in the street subsided, until the hurrying footsteps of the last belated straggler died away in the distance and left no sound behind.

The fire had burned low. A sense of loneliness crept over me. I arose and undressed, moving on tiptoe about the room, doing stealthily what I had to do, as if I were environed by sleeping enemies whose slumbers it would be fatal to break. I covered up in bed, and lay listening to the rain and wind and the faint creaking of distant shutters, till they lulled me to sleep.

I slept profoundly, but how long I do not know. All at once I found myself awake, and filled with a shuddering expectancy. All was still. All but my own heart—I could hear it beat. Presently the bedclothes began to slip away slowly toward the foot of the bed, as if some one were pulling them! I could not stir; I could not speak. Still the blankets slipped deliberately away, till my breast was uncovered. Then with a great effort I seized them and drew them over my head. I waited, listened, waited. Once more that steady pull began, and once more I lay torpid a century of dragging seconds till my breast was naked again. At last I roused my energies and snatched the covers back to their place and held them with a strong grip. I waited. By and by I felt a faint tug, and took a fresh grip. The tug strengthened to a steady strain—it grew stronger and stronger. My hold parted, and for the third time the blankets slid away. I groaned. An answering groan came from the foot of the bed! Beaded drops of sweat stood upon my forehead. I was more dead than alive. Presently I heard a heavy footstep in my room—the step of an elephant, it seemed to me—it was not like anything human. But it was moving *from* me—there was relief in that. I heard it approach the door—pass out without moving bolt or lock—and wander away among the dismal corridors, straining the floors and joists till they creaked again as it passed—and then silence reigned once more.

When my excitement had calmed, I said to myself, "This is a dream—simply a hideous dream." And so I lay thinking it over until I convinced myself that it *was* a dream, and then a comforting laugh relaxed my lips and I was happy again. I got up and struck a light; and when I found the locks and bolts were just as I had left them, another soothing laugh welled in my heart and rippled from my lips. I took my pipe and lit it, and was just sitting down before the fire, when—down went the pipe out of my nerveless fingers, the blood forsook my cheeks, and my placid breathing was cut short with a gasp! In the ashes on the hearth, side by side with my own bare footprint, was another, so vast that in comparison, mine was but an infant's! Then I *had* had a visitor, and the elephant tread was explained.

I put out the light and returned to bed, palsied with fear. I lay a long time, peering into the darkness, and listening.

Then I heard a grating noise overhead, like the dragging of a heavy body across the floor; then the throwing down of the body, and the shaking of my windows in response to the concussion. In distant parts of the building I heard the muffled slamming of doors. I heard, at intervals, stealthy footsteps creeping in and out among the corridors, and up and down the stairs. Sometimes these noises approached my door, hesitated, and went away again. I heard the clanking of chains faintly, in remote passages, and listened while the clanking grew nearer—while it wearily climbed the stairways, marking each move by the loose surplus of chain that fell with an accented rattle upon each succeeding step as the goblin that bore it advanced. I heard muttered sentences; half-uttered screams that seemed smothered violently; and the swish of invisible garments and the rush of invisible wings. Then I became conscious that my chamber was invaded—that I was not alone. I heard sighs and breathings about my bed, and mysterious whisperings. Three little spheres of phosphorescent light appeared on the ceiling directly over my head, clung and glowed there a moment, and then dropped—two of them upon my face and one upon the pillow. They spattered, liquidly, and felt warm. Intuition told me they had turned to gouts of blood as they fell—I needed no light to satisfy myself of that. Then I saw pallid faces, dimly luminous, and white uplifted hands, floating bodiless in the air—floating a moment and then disappearing. The whispering ceased, and the voices and the sounds, and a solemn stillness followed. I waited and listened. I felt that I must have light or die. I was weak with fear. I slowly raised myself toward a sitting posture, and my face came in contact with a clammy hand! All strength went from me apparently, and I fell back like a stricken invalid. Then I heard the rustle of a garment—it seemed to pass to the door and go out.

When everything was still once more, I crept out of bed, sick and feeble, and lit the gas with a hand that trembled as if it were aged with a hundred years. The light brought some little cheer to my spirits. I sat down and fell into a dreamy contemplation of that great footprint in the ashes. By and by its outlines began to waver and grow dim. I glanced up and the broad gas flame was slowly wilting away. In the same moment I heard that elephantine tread again. I noted its approach, nearer and nearer, along the musty halls, and dimmer and dimmer the light waned. The tread reached my very door and paused—the light had dwindled to a sickly blue, and all things about me were in a spectral twilight. The door did not open, and yet I felt a faint gust of air fan my cheek, and presently was conscious of a huge, cloudy presence before me. I watched it with fascinated eyes. A pale glow stole over the Thing; gradually its cloudy folds took shape—an arm appeared, then legs, then a body, and last a great sad face looked out of the vapor. Stripped of its filmy housings, naked, muscular and comely, the majestic Cardiff Giant loomed above me!

All my misery vanished—for a child might know that no harm could come with that benignant countenance. My cheerful spirits returned at once, and in sympathy with them the gas turned up brightly again. Never a lone outcast was so glad to welcome company as I was to greet the friendly giant. I said:

"Why, is it nobody but you? Do you know, I have been scared to death for the last two or three hours? I am most honestly glad to see you. I wish I had a chair—Here, here, don't try to sit down in that thing!"

But it was too late. He was in before I could stop him, and down he went—I never saw a chair shivered so in my life.

"Stop, stop, you'll ruin ev——"

Too late again. There was another crash, and another chair was resolved into its original elements.

"Confound it, haven't you got any judgment at all? Do you want to ruin all the furniture on the place? Here, here, you petrified fool——"

But it was no use. Before I could arrest him he had sat down on the bed, and it was a melancholy ruin.

"Now what sort of a way is that to do? First you come lumbering about the place bringing a legion of vagabond goblins along with you to worry me to death, and then, when I overlook an indelicacy of costume which would not be tolerated anywhere by cultivated people except in a respectable theater, and not even there if the nudity were of *your* sex, you repay me by wrecking all the furniture you can find to sit down on. And why will you? You damage yourself

as much as you do me. You have broken off the end of your
spinal column, and littered up the floor with chips of your
hands till the place looks like a marble yard. You ought to
be ashamed of yourself—you are big enough to know better."

"Well, I will not break any more furniture. But what am
I to do? I have not had a chance to sit down for a century."
And the tears came into his eyes.

"Poor devil," I said, "I should not have been so harsh
with you. And you are an orphan, too, no doubt. But sit
down on the floor here—nothing else can stand your weight
—and, besides, we cannot be sociable with you away up
there above me; I want you down where I can perch on this
high counting-house stool and gossip with you face to face."

So he sat down on the floor, and lit a pipe which I gave
him, threw one of my red blankets over his shoulders, in-
verted my sitz-bath on his head, helmet fashion, and made
himself picturesque and comfortable. Then he crossed his
ankles, while I renewed the fire, and exposed the flat,
honeycombed bottoms of his prodigious feet to the grateful
warmth.

"What is the matter with the bottom of your feet and the
back of your legs, that they are gouged up so?"

"Infernal chilblains—I caught them clear up to the back
of my head, roosting out there under Newell's farm. But I
love the place; I love it as one loves his old home. There is
no peace for me like the peace I feel when I am there."

We talked along for half an hour, and then I noticed that he looked tired, and I spoke of it.

"Tired?" he said. "Well, I should think so. And now I will tell you all about it, since you have treated me so well. I am the spirit of the Petrified Man that lies across the street there in the museum. I am the ghost of the Cardiff Giant. I can have no rest, no peace, till they have given that poor body burial again. Now what was the most natural thing for me to do, to make men satisfy this wish? Terrify them into it!—haunt the place where the body lay! So I haunted the museum night after night. I got the other spirits to help me. But it did no good, for nobody ever came to the museum at midnight. Then it occurred to me to come over the way and haunt this place a little. I felt that if I ever got a hearing I must succeed, for I had the most efficient company that tradition could furnish. Night after night we have shivered around through these mildewed halls, dragging chains, groaning, whispering, tramping up and down stairs, till, to tell you the truth, I am almost worn out. But when I saw a light in your room tonight, I roused my energies again and went at it with a deal of the old freshness. But I am tired out—entirely fagged out. Give me, I beseech you, give me some hope!"

I lit off my perch in a burst of excitement, and exclaimed:

"This transcends everything! Everything that ever did occur—why, you poor blundering old fossil, you have had all your trouble for nothing—you have been haunting a *plaster cast* of yourself—the real Cardiff Giant is in Albany! *

"Confound it, don't you know your own remains?"

I never saw such an eloquent look of shame, of pitiable humiliation, overspread a countenance before.

The Petrified Man rose slowly to his feet, and said:

"Honestly, *is* that true?"

"As true as I am sitting here."

He took the pipe from his mouth and laid it on the mantel, then stood irresolute a moment (unconsciously, from old habit, thrusting his hands where his pantaloon pockets should have been, and meditatively dropping his chin on his breast), and finally said:

"Well—I *never* felt so absurd before. The Petrified Man has sold everything else and now the mean fraud has ended by selling his own ghost! My son, if there is any charity left in your heart for a poor friendless phantom like me, don't let this get out. Think how *you* would feel if you had made such an ass of yourself."

I heard his stately tramp die away, step by step down the stairs and out into the deserted street, and felt sorry that he had gone, poor fellow—and sorrier still that he had carried off my red blanket and my bathtub.

* A fact. The original fraud was ingeniously and fraudfully duplicated, and exhibited in New York as the "only genuine" Cardiff Giant (to the unspeakable disgust of the owners of the real Colossus) at the very same time that the latter was drawing crowds at a museum in Albany.

THE SOUL
OF THE GREAT BELL
by Lafcadio Hearn

She leaped into the white flood of metal.

⤙ *Two*

THE water-clock marks the hour in the *Ta-chung sz'*—
in the Tower of the Great Bell: now the mallet is lifted to
smite the lips of the metal monster—the vast lips inscribed
with Buddhist texts from the sacred "Fa-hwa-King," from
the chapters of the holy "Ling-yen-King"! Hear the great
bell responding!—how mighty her voice, though tongue-
less!—KO-NGAI! All the little dragons on the high-tilted
eaves of the green roofs shiver to the tips of their gilded
tails under that deep wave of sound; all the porcelain gar-
goyles tremble on their carven perches; all the hundred little bells of the pagodas quiver with desire to speak. KO-
NGAI!—all the green-and-gold tiles of the temple are
vibrating; the wooden goldfish above them are writhing
against the sky; the uplifted finger of Fo shakes high over
the heads of the worshippers through the blue fog of in-
cense! KO-NGAI!—What a thunder tone was that! All the

lacquered goblins on the palace cornices wriggle their fire-colored tongues! And after each huge shock, how wondrous the multiple echo and the great golden moan and, at last, the sudden sibilant sobbing in the ears when the immense tone faints away in broken whispers of silver—as though a woman should whisper, *"Hiai!"* Even so the great bell hath sounded every day for well-nigh five hundred years—*Ko-Ngai:* first with stupendous clang, then with immeasurable moan of gold, then with silver murmuring of *"Hiai!"* And there is not a child in all the many-colored ways of the old Chinese city who does not know the story of the great bell —who cannot tell you why the great bell says *Ko-Ngai* and *Hiai!*

Now, this is the story of the great bell in the *Ta-chung sz',* as the same is related in the "Pe-Hiao-Tou-Choue," written by the learned Yu-Pao-Tchen, of the city of Kwang-tchau-fu.

Nearly five hundred years ago the Celestially August, the Son of Heaven, Yong-Lo, of the "Illustrious," or Ming, dynasty, commanded the worthy official Kouan-Yu that he should have a bell made of such size that the sound thereof might be heard for one hundred *li*. And he further ordained that the voice of the bell should be strengthened with brass, and deepened with gold, and sweetened with silver; and that the face and the great lips of it should be graven with blessed sayings from the sacred books, and that it should be suspended in the center of the imperial capital, to sound through all the many-colored ways of the city of Pe-king.

Therefore the worthy mandarin Kouan-Yu assembled the master-molders and the renowned bell-smiths of the empire, and all men of great repute and cunning in foundry work; and they measured the materials for the alloy, and treated them skillfully, and prepared the molds, the fires, the instruments, and the monstrous melting-pot for fusing the metal. And they labored exceedingly, like giants, neglecting only rest and sleep and the comforts of life; toiling both night and day in obedience to Kouan-Yu, and striving in all things to do the behest of the Son of Heaven.

But when the metal had been cast, and the earthen mold separated from the glowing casting, it was discovered that, despite their great labor and ceaseless care, the result was void of worth; for the metals had rebelled one against the other—the gold had scorned alliance with the brass, the silver would not mingle with the molten iron. Therefore the molds had to be once more prepared, and the metal remelted, and all the work tediously and toilsomely repeated. The Son of Heaven heard, and was angry, but spake nothing.

A second time the bell was cast, and the result was even worse. Still the metals obstinately refused to blend one with the other; and there was no uniformity in the bell, and the sides of it were cracked and fissured, and the lips of it were slagged and split asunder; so that all the labor had to be repeated even a third time, to the great dismay of Kouan-Yu. And when the Son of Heaven heard these things, he was angrier than before; and sent his messenger to Kouan-Yu

with a letter, written upon lemon-colored silk, and sealed
with the seal of the Dragon, containing these words:

*From the Mighty Yong-Lo, the Sublime Tait-Sung,
the Celestial and August—whose reign is called "Ming"
—to Kouan-Yu the Fuh-yin: Twice thou hast betrayed
the trust we have deigned graciously to place in thee;
if thou fail a third time in fulfilling our command, thy
head shall be severed from thy neck. Tremble and obey!*

Now, Kouan-Yu had a daughter of dazzling loveliness,
whose name—Ko-Ngai—was ever in the mouths of poets,
and whose heart was even more beautiful than her face.
Ko-Ngai loved her father with such love that she had refused
a hundred worthy suitors rather than make his home deso-
late by her absence; and when she had seen the awful yellow
missive, sealed with the Dragon-Seal, she fainted away with
fear for her father's sake. And when her senses and her
strength returned to her, she could not rest or sleep for
thinking of her parent's danger, until she had secretly sold
some of her jewels, and with the money so obtained had
hastened to an astrologer, and paid him a great price to advise her by what means her father might be saved from the
peril impending over him. So the astrologer made observa-
tions of the heavens, and marked the aspect of the Silver
Stream (which we call the Milky Way), and examined the
signs of the Zodiac—the *Hwang-tao,* or Yellow Road—and
consulted the table of the five *Hin,* or Principles of the Uni-

verse, and the mystical books of the alchemists. And after a long silence, he made answer to her, saying, "Gold and brass will never meet in wedlock, silver and iron will never embrace, until the flesh of a maiden be melted in the crucible; until the blood of a virgin be mixed with the metals in their fusion." So Ko-Ngai returned home sorrowful at heart; but she kept secret all that she had heard, and told no one what she had done.

At last came the awful day when the third and last effort to cast the great bell was to be made; and Ko-Ngai, together with her waiting-woman, accompanied her father to the foundry, and they took their places upon a platform overlooking the toiling of the molders and the lava of liquefied metal. All the workmen wrought their tasks in silence; there was no sound heard but the muttering of the fires. And the muttering deepened into a roar like the roar of typhoons approaching, and the blood-red lake of metal slowly brightened like the vermilion of a sunrise, and the vermilion was transmuted into a radiant glow of gold, and the gold whitened blindingly, like the silver face of a full moon. Then the workers ceased to feed the raving flame, and all fixed their eyes upon the eyes of Kouan-Yu; and Kouan-Yu prepared to give the signal to cast.

But ere ever he lifted his finger, a cry caused him to turn his head; and all heard the voice of Ko-Ngai sounding sharply sweet as a bird's song above the great thunder of the fires—*"For thy sake, O my father!"* And even as she cried, she leaped into the white flood of metal; and the lava

of the furnace roared to receive her, and spattered monstrous flakes of flame to the roof, and burst over the verge
of the earthen crater, and cast up a whirling fountain of
many-colored fires, and subsided quakingly, with lightnings
and with thunders and with mutterings.

Then the father of Ko-Ngai, wild with his grief, would
have leaped in after her, but that strong men held him back,
and kept firm grasp upon him until he had fainted away and
they could bear him like one dead to his home. And the
serving-woman of Ko-Ngai, dizzy and speechless for pain,
stood before the furnace, still holding in her hands a shoe,
a tiny, dainty shoe, with embroidery of pearls and flowers—
the shoe of her beautiful mistress that was. For she had
sought to grasp Ko-Ngai by the foot as she leaped, but had
only been able to clutch the shoe, and the pretty shoe came
off in her hand; and she continued to stare at it like one
gone mad.

But in spite of all these things, the command of the
Celestial and August had to be obeyed, and the work of the
molders to be finished, hopeless as the result might be.
Yet the glow of the metal seemed purer and whiter than
before; and there was no sign of the beautiful body that
had been entombed therein. So the ponderous casting was
made; and lo! when the metal had become cool, it was found
that the bell was beautiful to look upon, and perfect in
form, and wonderful in color above all other bells. Nor was
there any trace found of the body of Ko-Ngai; for it had
been totally absorbed by the precious alloy, and blended

with the well-blended brass and gold, with the intermingling of the silver and the iron. And when they sounded the bell, its tones were found to be deeper and mellower and mightier than the tones of any other bell—reaching even beyond the distance of one hundred *li,* like a pealing of summer thunder; and yet also like some vast voice uttering a name, a woman's name—the name of Ko-Ngai!

And still, between each mighty stroke, there is a long low moaning heard; and ever the moaning ends with a sound of sobbing and of complaining, as though a weeping woman should murmur *"Hiai!"* And still, when the people hear that great golden moan they keep silence; but when the sharp, sweet, shuddering comes in the air, and the sobbing of *"Hiai!"* then, indeed, do all the Chinese mothers in all the many-colored ways of Pe-king whisper to their little ones: *"Listen! that is Ko-Ngai crying for her shoe! That is Ko-Ngai calling for her shoe!"*

MY GRANDFATHER, HENDRY WATTY

by *Sir Arthur Quiller-Couch*

"Hendry Watty! Hendry Watty! pull me in."

⊱ *Three*

TIS the nicest miss in the world that I was born grandson of my own father's father, and not of another man altogether. Hendry Watty was the name of my grandfather that might have been; and he always maintained that to all intents and purposes he *was* my grandfather, and made me call him so—'twas such a narrow shave. I don't mind telling you about it. 'Tis a curious tale, too.

My grandfather, Hendry Watty, bet four gallons of eggy-hot that he would row out to the Shivering Grounds, all in the dead waste of the night, and haul a trammel there. To find the Shivering Grounds by night, you get the Gull Rock in a line with Tregamenna and pull out till you open the light on St. Anthony's Point; but everybody gives the place a wide berth because Archelaus Rowett's lugger foundered there, one time, with six hands on board; and they say that at night you can hear the drowned men hailing their names.

But my grandfather was the boldest man in Port Loe, and said he didn't care. So one Christmas Eve by daylight he and his mates went out and tilled the trammel; and then they came back and spent the forepart of the evening over the eggy-hot, down to Oliver's tiddly-wink, to keep my grandfather's spirits up and also to show that the bet was made in earnest.

'Twas past eleven o'clock when they left Oliver's and walked down to the cove to see my grandfather off. He has told me since that he didn't feel afraid at all, but very friendly in mind, especially toward William John Dunn, who was walking on his right hand. This puzzled him at first, for as a rule he didn't think much of William John Dunn. But now he shook hands with him several times, and just as he was stepping into the boat he says, "You'll take care of Mary Polly while I'm away." Mary Polly Polsue was my grandfather's sweetheart at that time. But why he should have spoken as if he was bound on a long voyage he never could tell; he used to set it down to fate.

"I will," said William John Dunn; and then they gave a cheer and pushed my grandfather off, and he lit his pipe and away he rowed all into the dead waste of the night. He rowed and rowed, all in the dead waste of the night; and he got the Gull Rock in a line with Tregamenna windows; and still he was rowing, when to his great surprise he heard a voice calling:

"Hendry Watty! Hendry Watty!"

I told you my grandfather was the boldest man in Port

Loe. But he dropped his two oars now, and made the five signs of Penitence. For who could it be calling him out here in the dead waste and middle of the night?

"HENDRY WATTY! HENDRY WATTY! *drop me a line.*"

My grandfather kept his fishing-lines in a little skivet under the stern-sheets. But not a trace of bait had he on board. If he had, he was too much a-tremble to bait a hook.

"HENDRY WATTY! HENDRY WATTY! *drop me a line, or I'll know why.*"

My poor grandfather by this had picked up his oars again, and was rowing like mad to get quit of the neighborhood, when something or somebody gave three knocks—*thump, thump, thump!*—on the bottom of the boat, just as you would knock on a door. The third thump fetched Hendry Watty upright on his legs. He had no more heart for disobeying, but having bitten his pipe-stem in half by this time—his teeth chattered so—he baited his hook with the broken bit and flung it overboard, letting the line run out in the stern-notch. Not halfway had it run before he felt a long pull on it, like the sucking of a dogfish.

"*Hendry Watty! Hendry Watty! pull me in.*"

Hendry Watty pulled in hand over fist, and in came the lead sinker over the notch, and still the line was heavy; he pulled and he pulled, and next, all out of the dead waste of the night, came two white hands, like a washerwoman's, and gripped hold of the stern-board; and on the left of these two hands, on the little finger, was a silver ring, sunk very deep in the flesh. If this was bad, worse was the face that followed—a great white parboiled face, with the hair and whiskers all stuck with chips of wood and seaweed. And if this was bad for anybody, it was worse for my grandfather, who had known Archelaus Rowett before he was drowned out on the Shivering Grounds, six years before.

Archelaus Rowett climbed in over the stern, pulled the hook with the bit of pipe-stem out of his cheek, sat down in the stern-sheets, shook a small crayfish out of his whiskers, and said very coolly:

"If you should come across my wife——"

That was all my grandfather stayed to hear. At the sound of Archelaus's voice he fetched a yell, jumped clean over the side of the boat and swam for dear life. He swam and swam, till by the bit of the moon he saw the Gull Rock close ahead. There were lashin's of rats on the Gull Rock, as he knew; but he was a good deal surprised at the way they were behaving, for they sat in a row at the water's edge and fished, with their tails let down into the sea for fishing-lines; and their eyes were like garnets burning as they looked at my grandfather over their shoulders.

"Hendry Watty! Hendry Watty! you can't land here—you're disturbing the pollack."

"Bejimbers! I wouldn' do that for the world," says my grandfather; so off he pushes and swims for the mainland. This was a long job, and 'twas as much as he could do to reach the Kibberick beach, where he fell on his face and hands among the stones, and there lay, taking breath.

The breath was hardly back in his body before he heard footsteps, and along the beach came a woman, and passed close by to him. He lay very quiet, and as she came near he saw 'twas Sarah Rowett, that used to be Archelaus's wife, but had married another man since. She was knitting as she went by, and did not seem to notice my grandfather; but he heard her say to herself, "The hour is come, and the man is come."

He had scarcely begun to wonder over this when he spied a ball of worsted yarn beside him that Sarah had dropped. 'Twas the ball she was knitting from, and a line of worsted stretched after her along the beach. Hendry Watty picked up the ball and followed the thread on tiptoe. In less than a minute he came near enough to watch what she was doing; and what she did was worth watching. First she gathered wreckwood and straw, and struck flint over touchwood and teened a fire. Then she unraveled her knitting; twisted her end of the yarn between finger and thumb—like a cobbler twisting a wax-end—and cast the end up towards the sky. It made Hendry Watty stare when the thread, instead of falling back to the ground, remained hanging, just as if 'twas fastened to something up above; but it made him stare more when Sarah Rowett began to climb up it, and away up till nothing could be seen of her but her ankles dangling out of the dead waste and middle of the night.

"HENDRY WATTY! HENDRY WATTY!"

It wasn't Sarah calling, but a voice far away out to sea. "HENDRY WATTY! HENDRY WATTY! *send me a line!*"

My grandfather was wondering what to do, when Sarah speaks down very sharp to him, out of the dark:

"Hendry Watty! where's the rocket apparatus? Can't you hear the poor fellow asking for a line?"

"I do," says my grandfather, who was beginning to lose his temper; "and do you think, ma'am, that I carry a Boxer's rocket in my trousers pocket?"

"I think you have a ball of worsted in your hand," says she. "Throw it as far as you can."

So my grandfather threw the ball out into the dead waste and middle of the night. He didn't see where it pitched, or how far it went.

"Right it is," says the woman aloft. " 'Tis easy seen you're a hurler. But what shall us do for a cradle! Hendry Watty! Hendry Watty!"

"Ma'am to *you*," says my grandfather.

"If you've the common feelings of a gentleman, I'll ask you kindly to turn your back; I'm going to take off my stocking."

So my grandfather stared the other way very politely; and when he was told he might look again, he saw she had tied the stocking to the line and was running it out like a cradle into the dead waste of the night.

"Hendry Watty! Hendry Watty! look out below."

Before he could answer, plump! a man's leg came tumbling past his ear and scattered the ashes right and left.

"Hendry Watty! Hendry Watty! look out below!"

This time 'twas a great white arm and hand, with a silver ring sunk tight in the flesh of the little finger.

"Hendry Watty! Hendry Watty! warm them limbs!"

My grandfather picked them up and was warming them before the fire, when down came tumbling a great round head and bounced twice and lay in the firelight, staring up at him. And whose head was it but Archelaus Rowett's, that he'd run away from once already that night.

"Hendry Watty! Hendry Watty! look out below!"

This time 'twas another leg, and my grandfather was just about to lay hands on it, when the woman called down:

"Hendry Watty! catch it quick! It's my own leg I've thrown down by mistake."

The leg struck the ground and bounced high, and Hendry Watty made a leap after it.

And I reckon it's asleep he must have been; for what he caught was not Mrs. Rowett's leg, but the jib-boom of a deep-laden brigantine that was running him down in the dark. And as he sprang for it, his boat was crushed by the brigantine's forefoot and went down under his very boot-soles. At the same time he let out a yell, and two or three of the crew ran forward and hoisted him up to the bowsprit and in on deck, safe and sound.

But the brigantine happened to be outward-bound for the River Plate; so that, what with one thing and another, 'twas eleven good months before my grandfather landed again at Port Loe. And who should be the first man he sees standing above the cove but William John Dunn?

"I'm very glad to see you," says William John Dunn.

"Thank you kindly," answers my grandfather; "and how's Mary Polly?"

"Why, as for that," he says, "she took so much looking after, that I couldn't feel I was keeping her properly under my eye till I married her, last June month."

"You was always one to overdo things," said my grandfather.

"But if you was alive an' well, why didn' you drop us a line?"

Now when it came to talk about "dropping a line" my grandfather fairly lost his temper. So he struck William John Dunn on the nose—a thing he had never been known to do before—and William John Dunn hit him back, and the neighbors had to separate them. And next day, William John Dunn took out a summons against him.

Well, the case was tried before the magistrate: and my grandfather told his story from the beginning, quite straightforward, just as I've told it to you. And the magistrates decided that, taking one thing with another, he'd had a great deal of provocation, and fined him five shillings. And there the matter ended. But now you know the reason why I'm William John Dunn's grandson instead of Hendry Watty's.

THE WATER GHOST OF HARROWBY HALL

by *John Kendrick Bangs*

These ends she drew across his forehead until he became like one insane.

Four

THE trouble with Harrowby Hall was that it was haunted, and, what was worse, the ghost did not content itself with merely appearing at the bedside of the afflicted person who saw it, but persisted in remaining there for one mortal hour before it would disappear.

It never appeared except on Christmas Eve, and then as the clock was striking twelve, in which respect alone was it lacking in that originality which in these days is a *sine qua non* of success in spectral life. The owners of Harrowby Hall had done their utmost to rid themselves of the damp and dewy lady who rose up out of the best bedroom floor at midnight, but without avail. They had tried to stop the clock, so that the ghost would not know when it was midnight; but she made her appearance just the same, with that fearful miasmatic personality of hers, and there she would stand until everything about her was thoroughly saturated.

Then the owners of Harrowby Hall calked up every crack in the floor with the very best quality of hemp, and over this were placed layers of tar and canvas; the walls were made waterproof, and the doors and windows likewise, the proprietors having conceived the notion that the unexorcised lady would find it difficult to leak into the room after these precautions had been taken; but even this did not suffice. The following Christmas Eve she appeared as promptly as before, and frightened the occupant of the room quite out of his senses by sitting down alongside of him and gazing with her cavernous blue eyes into his; and he noticed, too, that in her long, aqueously bony fingers bits of dripping seawood were entwined, the ends hanging down, and these ends she drew across his forehead until he became like one insane. And then he swooned away, and was found unconscious in his bed the next morning by his host, simply saturated with sea-water and fright, from the combined effects of which he never recovered, dying four years later of pneumonia and nervous prostration at the age of seventy-eight.

The next year the master of Harrowby Hall decided not to have the best spare bedroom opened at all, thinking that perhaps the ghost's thirst for making herself disagreeable would be satisfied by haunting the furniture, but the plan was as unavailing as the many that had preceded.

The ghost appeared as usual in the room—that is, it was supposed she did, for the hangings were dripping wet the next morning, and in the parlor below the haunted room a great damp spot appeared on the ceiling. Finding no one there, she immediately set out to learn the reason why, and she chose none other to haunt than the owner of the Harrowby himself. She found him in his own cozy room drinking whiskey—whiskey undiluted—and felicitating himself upon having foiled her ghostship, when all of a sudden the curl went out of his hair, his whiskey bottle filled and overflowed, and he was himself in a condition similar to that of a man who had fallen into a water-butt. When he had recovered from the shock, which was a painful one, he saw before him the lady of the cavernous eyes and the seaweed fingers. The sight was so unexpected and so terrifying that he fainted, but immediately came to, because of the vast amount of water in his hair, which, trickling down over his face, restored his consciousness.

Now it so happened that the master of Harrowby was a brave man, and while he was not particularly fond of interviewing ghosts, especially such quenching ghosts as the one before him, he was not to be daunted by an apparition. He had paid the lady the compliment of fainting from the effects of his first surprise, and now that he had come to, he intended to find out a few things he felt he had a right to know. He would have liked to put on a dry suit of clothes first, but the apparition declined to leave him for an instant until her hour was up, and he was forced to deny himself that pleasure. Every time he would move she would follow him, with the result that everything she came in contact with got a ducking. In an effort to warm himself up, he approached the fire, an unfortunate move as it turned out, because it brought the ghost directly over the fire, which immediately was extinguished. The whiskey became utterly valueless as a comforter to his chilled system, because it was by this time diluted to a proportion of ninety per cent of water. The only thing he could do to ward off the evil effects of his encounter he did, and that was to swallow ten two-grain quinine pills, which he managed to put into his mouth before the ghost had time to interfere. Having done this, he turned with some asperity to the ghost, and said:

"Far be it from me to be impolite to a woman, madam, but I'm hanged if it wouldn't please me better if you'd stop these infernal visits of yours to this house. Go sit out on the lake, if you like that sort of thing; soak the water-butt, if you wish; but do not, I implore you, come into a gentleman's house and saturate him and his possessions in this way. It is disagreeable."

"Henry Hartwick Oglethorpe," said the ghost, in a gurgling voice, "you don't know what you are talking about."

"Madam," returned the unhappy householder, "I wish that remark were strictly truthful. I was talking about you. It would be shillings and pence—nay, pounds, in my pocket, madam, if I did not know you."

"That is a bit of specious nonsense," returned the ghost, throwing a quart of indignation into the face of the master of Harrowby. "It may rank high as repartee, but as a comment upon my statement that you do not know what you are talking about, it savors of irrelevant impertinence. You do not know that I am compelled to haunt this place year after year by inexorable fate. It is no pleasure to me to enter this house, and ruin and mildew everything I touch. I never aspired to be a shower-bath, but it is my doom. Do you know who I am?"

"No, I don't," returned the master of Harrowby. "I should say you were the Lady of the Lake, or Little Sallie Waters."

"You are a witty man for your years," said the ghost.

"Well, my humor is drier than yours will ever be," returned the master.

"No doubt. I'm never dry. I am the Water Ghost of Harrowby Hall, and dryness is a quality entirely beyond my wildest hope. I have been the incumbent of this highly unpleasant office for two hundred years tonight."

"How the deuce did you ever come to get elected?" asked the master.

"Through a suicide," replied the specter. "I am the ghost of that fair maiden whose picture hangs over the mantelpiece in the drawing-room. I should have been your great-great-great-great-great-aunt if I had lived, Henry Hartwick Oglethorpe, for I was the own sister of your great-great-great-great-grandfather."

"But what induced you to get this house into such a predicament?"

"I was not to blame, sir," returned the lady. "It was my father's fault. He it was who built Harrowby Hall, and the haunted chamber was to have been mine. My father had it furnished in pink and yellow, knowing well that blue and gray formed the only combination of color I could tolerate. He did it merely to spite me, and with what I deem a proper spirit, I declined to live in the room; whereupon my father said I could live there or on the lawn, he didn't care which. That night I ran from the house and jumped over the cliff into the sea."

"That was rash," said the master of Harrowby.

"So I've heard," returned the ghost. "If I had known what the consequences were to be I should not have jumped; but I really never realized what I was doing until after I was drowned. I had been drowned a week when a sea-nymph came to me and informed me that I was to be one of her followers forever afterwards, adding that it should be my doom to haunt Harrowby Hall for one hour every Christmas Eve throughout the rest of eternity. I was to haunt that room on such Christmas Eves as I found it inhabited; and if it should turn out not to be inhabited, I was and am to spend the allotted hour with the head of the house."

"I'll sell the place."

"That you cannot do, for it is also required of me that I shall appear as the deeds are to be delivered to any purchaser, and divulge to him the awful secret of the house."

"Do you mean to tell me that on every Christmas Eve that I don't happen to have somebody in that guest-chamber, you are going to haunt me wherever I may be, ruining my whiskey, taking all the curl out of my hair, extinguishing my fire, and soaking me through to the skin?" demanded the master.

"You have stated the case, Oglethorpe. And what is more," said the water ghost, "it doesn't make the slightest difference where you are; if I find that room empty, wherever you may be I shall douse you with my spectral pres——"

Here the clock struck one, and immediately the apparition faded away. It was perhaps more of a trickle than a fade, but as a disappearance it was complete.

"By Saint George and his Dragon!" ejaculated the master of Harrowby, wringing his hands. "It is guineas to hot cross buns that next Christmas there's an occupant of the spare room, or I spend the night in a bathtub."

But the master of Harrowby would have lost his wager had there been any one there to take him up, for when Christmas Eve came again he was in his grave, never having recovered from the cold contracted that awful night. Harrowby Hall was closed, and the heir to the estate was in London, where to him in his chambers came the same experience that his father had gone through, saving only that, being younger and stronger, he survived the shock. Everything in his room was ruined—his clocks were rusted in the works; a fine collection of water-color drawings was entirely obliterated by the onslaught of the water ghost; and, what was worse, the apartments below his were drenched with the water soaking through the floors, a damage for which he was compelled to pay, and which resulted in his being requested by his landlady to vacate the premises immediately.

The story of the visitation inflicted upon his family had gone abroad, and no one could be got to invite him out to any function save afternoon teas and receptions. Fathers of daughters declined to permit him to remain in their houses later than eight o'clock at night, not knowing but that some emergency might arise in the supernatural world which would require the unexpected appearance of the water ghost in this on nights other than Christmas Eve, and before the mystic hour when weary churchyards, ignoring the rules which are supposed to govern polite society, begin to yawn. Nor would the maids themselves have aught to do with him, fearing the destruction by the sudden incursion of aqueous femininity of the costumes which they held most dear.

So the heir of Harrowby Hall resolved, as his ancestors for several generations before him had resolved, that something must be done. His first thought was to make one of his servants occupy the haunted room at the crucial moment; but in this he failed, because the servants themselves knew the history of the room and rebelled. None of his friends would consent to sacrifice their personal comfort to his, nor was there to be found in all England a man so poor as to be willing to occupy the doomed chamber on Christmas Eve for pay.

Then the thought came to the heir to have the fireplace in the room enlarged, so that he might evaporate the ghost at its first appearance, and he was felicitating himself upon the ingenuity of his plan, when he remembered what his father had told him—how that no fire could withstand the lady's extremely contagious dampness. And then he bethought him of steampipes. These, he remembered, could lie hundreds of feet deep in water, and still retain sufficient heat to drive the water away in vapor; and as a result of this thought the haunted room was heated by steam to a withering degree, and the heir for six months attended daily the Turkish baths, so that when Christmas Eve came he could himself withstand the awful temperature of the room.

The scheme was only partially successful. The water ghost appeared at the specified time, and found the heir of Harrowby prepared; but hot as the room was, it shortened her visit by no more than five minutes in the hour, during which time the nervous system of the young master was well-nigh shattered, and the room itself was cracked and warped to an extent which required the outlay of a large sum of money to remedy. And worse than this, as the last drop of the water ghost was slowly sizzling itself out on the floor, she whispered to her would-be conqueror that his scheme would avail him nothing, because there was still water in great plenty where she came from, and that next year would find her rehabilitated and as exasperatingly saturating as ever.

It was then that the natural action of the mind, in going from one extreme to the other, suggested to the ingenious heir of Harrowby the means by which the water ghost was ultimately conquered, and happiness once more came within the grasp of the house of Oglethorpe.

The heir provided himself with a warm suit of fur underclothing. Donning this with the furry side in, he placed over it a rubber garment, tight-fitting, which he wore just as a woman wears a jersey. On top of this he placed another set of underclothing, this suit made of wool, and over this was a second rubber garment like the first. Upon his head he placed a light and comfortable diving helmet, and so clad, on the following Christmas Eve he awaited the coming of his tormentor.

It was a bitterly cold night that brought to a close this twenty-fourth day of December. The air outside was still, but the temperature was below zero. Within all was quiet, the servants of Harrowby Hall awaiting with beating hearts the outcome of their master's campaign against his supernatural visitor.

The master himself was lying on the bed in the haunted room, clad as has already been indicated, and then——

The clock clanged out the hour of twelve.

There was a sudden banging of doors, a blast of cold air swept through the halls, the door leading into the haunted chamber flew open, a splash was heard, and the water ghost was seen standing at the side of the heir of Harrowby, from whose outer dress there streamed rivulets of water, but whose own person deep down under the various garments he wore was as dry and as warm as he could have wished.

"Ha!" said the young master of Harrowby. "I'm glad to see you."

"You are the most original man I've met, if that is true," returned the ghost. "May I ask where did you get that hat?"

"Certainly, madam," returned the master, courteously.

"It is a little portable observatory I had made just for such emergencies as this. But, tell me, is it true that you are doomed to follow me about for one mortal hour—to stand where I stand, to sit where I sit?"

"That is my delectable fate," returned the lady.

"We'll go out on the lake," said the master, starting up.

"You can't get rid of me that way," returned the ghost. "The water won't swallow me up; in fact, it will just add to my present bulk."

"Nevertheless," said the master firmly, "we will go out on the lake."

"But, my dear sir," returned the ghost, with a pale reluctance, "it is fearfully cold out there. You will be frozen hard before you've been out ten minutes."

"Oh, no, I'll not," replied the master. "I am very warmly dressed. Come!" This last in a tone of command that made the ghost ripple.

And they started.

They had not gone far before the water ghost showed signs of distress.

"You walk too slowly," she said. "I am nearly frozen. My knees are so stiff now I can hardly move. I beseech you to accelerate your step."

"I should like to oblige a lady," returned the master courteously, "but my clothes are rather heavy, and a hundred yards an hour is about my speed. Indeed, I think we would better sit down here on this snowdrift, and talk matters over."

"Do not! Do not do so, I beg!" cried the ghost. "Let me move on. I feel myself growing rigid as it is. If we stop here, I shall be frozen stiff."

"That, madam," said the master slowly, and seating himself on an ice-cake—"that is why I have brought you here. We have been on this spot just ten minutes; we have fifty more. Take your time about it, madam, but freeze, that is all I ask of you."

"I cannot move my right leg now," cried the ghost, in despair, "and my overskirt is a solid sheet of ice. Oh, good, kind Mr. Oglethorpe, light a fire, and let me go free from these icy fetters."

"Never, madam. It cannot be. I have you at last."

"Alas!" cried the ghost, a tear trickling down her frozen cheek. "Help me, I beg. I congeal."

"Congeal, madam, congeal!" returned Oglethorpe coldly. "You have drenched me and mine for two hundred and three years, madam. Tonight you have had your last drench."

"Ah, but I shall thaw out again, and then you'll see. Instead of the comfortably tepid, genial ghost I have been in my past, sir, I shall be iced-water," cried the lady threateningly.

"No, you won't, either," returned Oglethorpe; "for when you are frozen quite stiff, I shall send you to a cold-storage warehouse, and there shall you remain an icy work of art forever more."

"But warehouses burn."

"So they do, but this warehouse cannot burn. It is made of asbestos and surrounding it are fireproof walls, and within those walls the temperature is now and shall forever be 416 degrees below the zero point; low enough to make an icicle of any flame in the world—or the next," the master added, with an ill-suppressed chuckle.

"For the last time let me beseech you. I would go on my knees to you, Oglethorpe, were they not already frozen. I beg of you do not doo——"

Here even the words froze on the water ghost's lips and the clock struck one. There was a momentary tremor throughout the ice-bound form, and the moon, coming out from behind a cloud, shone down on the rigid figure of a beautiful woman sculptured in clear, transparent ice. There stood the ghost of Harrowby Hall, conquered by the cold, a prisoner for all time.

The heir of Harrowby had won at last, and today in a large storage house in London stands the frigid form of one who will never again flood the house of Oglethorpe with woe and sea-water.

As for the heir of Harrowby, his success in coping with a ghost has made him famous, a fame that still lingers about him, although his victory took place some twenty years ago; and so far from being unpopular with the fair sex, as he was when we first knew him, he has not only been married twice, but is to lead a third bride to the altar before the year is out.

THE BOLD DRAGOON

or

THE ADVENTURE OF MY GRANDFATHER

by Washington Irving

The musician now played fiercer and fiercer, and bobbed his head and his nightcap about like mad.

⊱ *Five*

My grandfather was a bold dragoon, for it's a profession, d'ye see, that has run in the family. All my forefathers have been dragoons and died upon the field of honor except myself, and I hope my posterity may be able to say the same; however, I don't mean to be vainglorious. Well, my grandfather, as I said, was a bold dragoon, and had served in the Low Countries. In fact, he was one of that very army, which, according to my uncle Toby, "swore so terribly in Flanders." He could swear a good stick himself; and, moreover, was the very man that introduced the doctrine Corporal Trim mentions, of radical heat and radical moisture; or, in other words, the mode of keeping out the damps of ditch water by burnt brandy. Be that as it may, it's nothing to the purport of my story. I only tell it to show you that my grandfather was a man not easily to be humbugged. He had seen service; or, according to his own phrase, "he had seen the divil"—and that's saying everything.

Well, gentlemen, my grandfather was on his way to England, for which he intended to embark at Ostend—bad luck to the place for one where I was kept by storms and head winds for three long days, and the divil of a jolly companion or pretty face to comfort me. Well, as I was saying, my grandfather was on his way to England, or rather to Ostend—no matter which, it's all the same. So one evening, towards nightfall, he rode jollily into Bruges. Very like you all know Bruges, gentlemen, a queer, old-fashioned Flemish town, once they say a great place for trade and money-making, in old times, when the Mynheers were in their glory; but almost as large and as empty as an Irishman's pocket at the present day. Well, gentlemen, it was the time of the annual fair. All Bruges was crowded; and the canals swarmed with Dutch boats, and the streets swarmed with Dutch merchants; and there was hardly any getting along for goods, wares, and merchandises, and peasants in big breeches, and women in half a score of petticoats.

My grandfather rode jollily along, in his easy, slashing way, for he was a saucy, sunshiny fellow—staring about him at the motley crowd, and the old houses with gable ends to the street and storks' nests on the chimneys; winking at the ya vrouws who showed their faces at the windows, and joking the women right and left in the street; all of whom laughed and took it in amazing good part; for though he did not know a word of their language, yet he had always a knack of making himself understood among the women.

Well, gentlemen, it being the time of the annual fair, all

the town was crowded; every inn and tavern full, and my grandfather applied in vain from one to the other for admittance. At length he rode up to an old rackety inn that looked ready to fall to pieces, and which all the rats would have run away from, if they could have found room in any other house to put their heads. It was just such a queer building as you see in Dutch pictures, with a tall roof that reached up into the clouds; and as many garrets, one over the other, as the seven heavens of Mahomet. Nothing had saved it from tumbling down but a stork's nest on the chimney, which always brings good luck to a house in the Low Countries; and at the very time of my grandfather's arrival, there were two of these long-legged birds of grace, standing like ghosts on the chimney top. Faith, but they've kept the house on its legs to this very day; for you may see it any time you pass through Bruges, as it stands there yet; only it is turned into a brewery—a brewery of strong Flemish beer; at least it was so when I came that way after the battle of Waterloo.

My grandfather eyed the house curiously as he approached. It might not altogether have struck his fancy, had he not seen in large letters over the door,

HEER VERKOOPT MAN GOEDEN DRANK

My grandfather had learnt enough of the language to know that the sign promised good liquor. "This is the house for me," said he, stopping short before the door.

The sudden appearance of a dashing dragoon was an event in an old inn, frequented only by the peaceful sons of traffic. A rich burgher of Antwerp, a stately ample man, in a broad Flemish hat, and who was the great man and great patron of the establishment, sat smoking a clean long pipe on one side of the door; a fat distiller of Geneva from Schiedam sat smoking on the other, and the bottle-nosed host stood in the door, and the comely hostess, in crimped cap, beside him, and the hostess' daughter, a plump Flanders lass, with long gold pendants in her ears, was at a side window.

"Humph!" said the rich burgher of Antwerp, with a sulky glance at the stranger.

"Der duyvel!" said the fat little distiller of Schiedam.

The landlord saw with the quick glance of a publican that the new guest was not at all, at all, to the taste of the old ones; and to tell the truth, he did not himself like my grandfather's saucy eye. He shook his head—not a garret in the house but was full.

"Not a garret!" echoed the landlady.

"Not a garret!" echoed the daughter.

The burgher of Antwerp and the little distiller of Schiedam continued to smoke their pipes sullenly, eyed the enemy askance from under their broad hats, but said nothing.

My grandfather was not a man to be browbeaten. He threw the reins on his horse's neck, cocked his hat on one side, stuck one arm akimbo, slapped his broad thigh with the other hand——

"Faith and troth!" said he, "but I'll sleep in this house this very night!"

My grandfather had on a tight pair of buckskins—the slap went to the landlady's heart.

He followed up the vow by jumping off his horse, and making his way past the staring Mynheers into the public room. May be you've been in the barroom of an old Flemish inn—faith, but a handsome chamber it was as you'd wish to see; with a brick floor, a great fireplace, with the whole Bible history in glazed tiles; and then the mantelpiece, pitching itself head foremost out of the wall, with a whole regiment of cracked teapots and earthen jugs paraded on it; not to mention half a dozen great Delft platters hung about the room by way of pictures; and the little bar in one corner, and the bouncing barmaid inside of it with a red calico cap and yellow eardrops.

My grandfather snapped his fingers over his head, as he cast an eye round the room. "Faith, this is the very house I've been looking after," said he.

There was some further show of resistance on the part of the garrison, but my grandfather was an old soldier, and an Irishman to boot, and not easily repulsed, especially after he had got into the fortress. So he blarney'd the landlord, kissed the landlord's wife, tickled the landlord's daughter, chucked the barmaid under the chin; and it was agreed on all hands that it would be a thousand pities, and a burning shame into the bargain, to turn such a bold dragoon into the streets. So they laid their heads together, that is to say, my grandfather and the landlady, and it was at length agreed to accommodate him with an old chamber that had for some time been shut up.

"Some say it's haunted!" whispered the landlord's daughter, "but you're a bold dragoon, and I dare say don't fear ghosts."

"The divil a bit!" said my grandfather, pinching her plump cheek; "but if I should be troubled by ghosts, I've been to the Red Sea in my time, and have a pleasant way of laying them, my darling!"

And then he whispered something to the girl which made her laugh, and give him a good-humored box on the ear. In short, there was nobody knew better how to make his way among the petticoats than my grandfather.

In a little while, as was his usual way, he took complete possession of the house; swaggering all over it—into the stable to look after his horse; into the kitchen to look after his supper. He had something to say or do with every one; smoked with the Dutchmen; drank with the Germans; slapped the men on the shoulders, tickled the women under the ribs—never since the days of Ally Croaker had such a rattling blade been seen. The landlord stared at him with astonishment; the landlord's daughter hung her head and giggled whenever he came near; and as he turned his back and swaggered along, his tight jacket setting off his broad shoulders and plump buckskins, and his long sword trailing by his side, the maids whispered to one another—"What a proper man!"

At supper my grandfather took command of the table d'hôte as though he had been at home; helped everybody, not forgetting himself; talked with every one, whether he understood their language or not; and made his way into the intimacy of the rich burgher of Antwerp, who had never been known to be sociable with any one during his life. In fact, he revolutionized the whole establishment, and gave it such a rouse, that the very house reeled with it. He outsat every one at table excepting the little fat distiller of Schiedam, who had sat soaking for a long time before he broke forth; but when he did, he was a very devil incarnate. He took a violent affection for my grandfather; so they sat drinking, and smoking, and telling stories, and singing Dutch and Irish songs, without understanding a word each other said, until the little Hollander was fairly swamped with his own gin and water, and carried off to bed, whooping and hiccuping, and trolling the burthen of a Low Dutch love song.

Well, gentlemen, my grandfather was shown to his quarters, up a huge staircase composed of loads of hewn timber; and through long rigmarole passages, hung with blackened paintings of fruit, and fish, and game, and country frolics, and huge kitchens, and portly burgomasters, such as you see about old-fashioned Flemish inns, till at length he arrived at his room.

An old-times chamber it was, sure enough, and crowded with all kinds of trumpery. It looked like an infirmary for decayed and superannuated furniture, where everything diseased and disabled was sent to nurse, or to be forgotten. Or rather, it might have been taken for a general congress of old legitimate movables, where every kind and country had a representative. No two chairs were alike; such high backs and low backs, and leather bottoms, and worsted bottoms, and straw bottoms, and no bottoms; and cracked marble tables with curiously carved legs, holding balls in their claws, as though they were going to play at ninepins.

My grandfather made a bow to the motley assemblage as he entered, and having undressed himself, placed his light in the fireplace, asking pardon of the tongs, which seemed to be making love to the shovel in the chimney corner, and whispering soft nonsense in its ear.

The rest of the guests were by this time sound asleep; for your Mynheers are huge sleepers. The housemaids, one by one, crept yawning to their attics, and not a female head in the inn was laid on a pillow that night without dreaming of the Bold Dragoon.

My grandfather, for his part, got into bed, and drew over him one of those great bags of down, under which they smother a man in the Low Countries; and there he lay, melting between two feather beds, like an anchovy sandwich between two slices of toast and butter. He was a warm-complexioned man, and this smothering played the very deuce with him. So, sure enough, in a little while it seemed as if a legion of imps were twitching at him, and all the blood in his veins was in fever heat.

He lay still, however, until all the house was quiet, excepting the snoring of the Mynheers from the different chambers; who answered one another in all kinds of tones and cadences, like so many bullfrogs in a swamp. The quieter the house became, the more unquiet became my grandfather. He waxed warmer and warmer, until at length the bed became too hot to hold him.

"Faith, there's no standing this any longer," says he; so he jumped out of bed and went strolling about the house.

Well, my grandfather had been for some time absent from his room, and was returning, perfectly cool, when just as he reached the door he heard a strange noise within. He paused and listened. It seemed as if some one was trying to hum a tune in defiance of the asthma. He recollected the report of the room's being haunted; but he was no believer in ghosts. So he pushed the door gently ajar, and peeped in.

Egad, gentlemen, there was a gambol carrying on within enough to have astonished St. Anthony.

By the light of the fire he saw a pale, weazen-faced fellow in a long flannel gown and a tall white nightcap with a tassel to it, who sat by the fire, with a bellows under his arm by way of bagpipe, from which he forced the asthmatical music that had bothered my grandfather. As he played, too, he kept twitching about with a thousand queer contortions; nodding his head and bobbing about his tasselled nightcap.

My grandfather thought this very odd, and mighty presumptuous and was about to demand what business he had to play his wind instruments in another gentleman's quarters, when a new cause of astonishment met his eye. From the opposite side of the room a long-backed, dandy-legged chair, covered with leather, and studded all over in a cox-comical fashion with little brass nails, got suddenly into motion; thrust out first a claw foot, then a crooked arm, and at length, making a leg, slid gracefully up to an easy chair of tarnished brocade, with a hole in its bottom, and led it gallantly out in a ghostly minuet about the floor.

The musician now played fiercer and fiercer, and bobbed his head and his nightcap about like mad. By degrees the dancing mania seemed to seize upon all the other pieces of furniture. The antique, long-bodied chairs paired off in couples and led down a country dance; a three-legged stool danced a hornpipe, though horribly puzzled by its supernumerary leg; while the amorous tongs seized the shovel around the waist and whirled it about the room in a German waltz. In short, all the movables got in motion, capering about; pirouetting, hands across, right and left, like so many devils, all except the clothes-press, which kept curtseying and curtseying, like a dowager, in one corner, in exquisite time to the music—being either too corpulent to dance, or perhaps at a loss for a partner.

My grandfather concluded the latter to be the reason; so, being, like a true Irishman, devoted to the sex, and at all times ready for a frolic, he bounced into the room, calling to the musicians to strike up "Paddy O'Rafferty," capered up to the clothes-press and seized upon two handles to lead her out—when, whizz!—the whole revel was at an end. The chairs, tables, tongs, and shovel slunk in an instant as quietly into their places as if nothing had happened; and the musician vanished up the chimney, leaving the bellows behind him in his hurry. My grandfather found himself seated in the middle of the floor, with the clothes-press sprawling before him, and the two handles jerked off and in his hands.

Well, gentlemen, as the clothes-press was a mighty heavy body, and my grandfather likewise, particularly in the rear, you may easily suppose two such heavy bodies coming to the ground would make a bit of noise. Faith, the old mansion shook as though it had mistaken it for an earthquake. The whole garrison was alarmed. The landlord, who slept just below, hurried up with a candle to inquire the cause, but with all his haste his daughter had hurried to the scene of uproar before him. The landlord was followed by the land-lady, who was followed by the bouncing barmaid, who was followed by the simpering chambermaids all holding together, as well as they could, such garments as they had first laid hands on; but all in a terrible hurry to see what the devil was to pay in the chamber of the Bold Dragoon.

My grandfather related the marvelous scene he had witnessed, and the prostrate clothes-press and the broken handles bore testimony to the fact. There was no contesting such evidence; particularly with a lad of my grandfather's complexion, who seemed able to make good every word either with sword or shillelah. So the landlord scratched his head and looked silly, as he was apt to do when puzzled. The landlady scratched—no, she did not scratch her head—but she knit her brow, and did not seem half pleased with the explanation. But the landlady's daughter corroborated it by recollecting that the last person who had dwelt in that chamber was a famous juggler who had died of St. Vitus's dance, and no doubt had infected all the furniture.

This set all things to rights, particularly when the chambermaids declared that they had all witnessed strange carryings on in that room—and as they declared this "upon their honors," there could not remain a doubt upon the subject.

PETER RUGG,
THE MISSING MAN
by William Austin

He was driving at great speed, as though he expected to outstrip the tempest.

⊱ *Six*

F<small>ROM</small> Jonathan Dunwell, of New York, to Mr. Herman Krauff.

Sir—Agreeably to my promise, I now relate to you all the particulars of the lost man and child which I have been able to collect. It is entirely owing to the humane interest you seemed to take in the report that I have pursued the inquiry to the following result.

You may remember that business called me to Boston in the summer of 1820. I sailed in the packet to Providence, and when I arrived there I learned that every seat in the stage was engaged. I was thus obliged either to wait a few hours or accept a seat with the driver, who civilly offered me that accommodation. Accordingly, I took my seat by his side, and soon found him intelligent and communicative. When we had traveled about ten miles, the horses suddenly threw their ears on their necks, as flat as a hare's. Said the driver, "Have you a surtout with you?"

"No," said I; "why do you ask?"

"You will want one soon," said he. "Do you observe the ears of all the horses?"

"Yes; and was just about to ask the reason."

"They see the storm-breeder, and we shall see him soon."

At this moment there was not a cloud visible in the firmament. Soon after, a small speck appeared in the road.

"There," said my companion, "comes the storm-breeder. He always leaves a Scotch mist behind him. By many a wet jacket do I remember him. I suppose the poor fellow suffers much himself—much more than is known to the world."

Presently a man with a child beside him, with a large black horse, and a weather-beaten chair, once built for a chaise-body, passed in great haste, apparently at the rate of twelve miles an hour. He seemed to grasp the reins of his horse with firmness, and appeared to anticipate his speed. He seemed dejected, and looked anxiously at the passengers, particularly at the stage-driver and myself. In a moment after he passed us, the horses' ears were up, and bent themselves forward so that they nearly met.

"Who is that man?" said I. "He seems in great trouble."

"Nobody knows who he is, but his person and the child are familiar to me. I have met him more than a hundred times, and have been so often asked the way to Boston by that man, even when he was traveling directly from that town, that of late I have refused any communication with him; and that is the reason he gave me such a fixed look."

"But does he never stop anywhere?"

"I have never known him to stop anywhere longer than to inquire the way to Boston; and let him be where he may, he will tell you he cannot stay a moment, for he must reach Boston that night."

We were now ascending a high hill in Walpole; and as we had a fair view of the heavens, I was rather disposed to jeer the driver for thinking of his surtout, as not a cloud as big as a marble could be discerned.

"Do you look," said he, "in the direction whence the man came; that is the place to look. The storm never meets him; it follows him."

We presently approached another hill; and when at the height, the driver pointed out in an eastern direction a little black speck about as big as a hat. "There," said he, "is the seed-storm. We may possibly reach Polley's before it reaches us, but the wanderer and his child will go to Providence through rain, thunder, and lightning."

And now the horses, as though taught by instinct, hastened with increased speed. The little black cloud came on rolling over the turnpike, and doubled and trebled itself in all directions. The appearance of this cloud attracted the notice of all the passengers, for, after it had spread itself to a great bulk, it suddenly became more limited in circumference, grew more compact, dark, and consolidated. And now the successive flashes of chain lightning caused the whole cloud to appear like a sort of irregular network, and displayed a thousand fantastic images. The driver bespoke my attention to a remarkable configuration in the cloud. He said every flash of lightning near its center discovered to him, distinctly, the form of a man sitting in an open carriage drawn by a black horse. But in truth I saw no such thing; the man's fancy was doubtless at fault. It is very common for the imagination to paint for the senses, both in the visible and invisible world.

In the meantime the distant thunder gave notice of a shower at hand; and just as we reached Polley's tavern the rain poured down in torrents. It was soon over, the cloud passing in the direction of the turnpike towards Providence. In a few moments after, a respectable-looking man in a chaise stopped at the door. The man and child in the chair having excited some little sympathy among the passengers, the gentleman was asked if he had observed them. He said he had met them; that the man seemed bewildered, and inquired the way to Boston; that he was driving at great speed, as though he expected to outstrip the tempest; that the moment he had passed him, a thunderclap broke directly over the man's head, and seemed to envelop both man and child, horse and carriage. "I stopped," said the gentleman, "supposing the lightning had struck him, but the horse only seemed to loom up and increase his speed; and as well as I could judge, he traveled just as fast as the thundercloud."

While this man was speaking, a peddler with a cart of tin merchandise came up, all dripping; and on being questioned, he said he had met that man and carriage, within a fortnight, in four different states; that at each time he had inquired the way to Boston; and that a thunder-shower like the present had each time deluged his wagon and his wares, setting his tin pots, etc., afloat, so that he had determined to get a marine insurance for the future. But that which excited his surprise most was the strange conduct of his horse, for long before he could distinguish the man in the chair, his own horse stood still in the road, and flung back his ears. "In short," said the peddler, "I wish never to see that man and horse again; they do not look to me as though they belonged to this world."

This was all I could learn at that time; and the occurrence soon after would have become with me "like one of those things which had never happened," had I not, as I stood recently on the doorstep of Bennett's Hotel in Hartford, heard a man say, "There goes Peter Rugg and his child! he looks wet and weary, and farther from Boston than ever." I was satisfied it was the same man I had seen more than three years before; for whoever has once seen Peter Rugg can never after be deceived as to his identity.

"Peter Rugg!" said I; "and who is Peter Rugg?"

"That," said the stranger, "is more than any one can tell exactly. He is a famous traveler, held in light esteem by all innholders, for he never stops to eat, drink or sleep. I wonder why the government does not employ him to carry the mail."

"Ay," said a bystander, "that is a thought bright only on one side; how long would it take in that case to send a letter to Boston, for Peter has already, to my knowledge, been more than twenty years traveling to that place."

"But," said I, "does the man never stop anywhere? Does he never converse with any one? I saw the same man more than three years since, near Providence, and I heard a strange story about him. Pray, sir, give me some account of this man."

"Sir," said the stranger, "those who know the most respecting that man say the least. I have heard it asserted that Heaven sometimes sets a mark on a man, either for judgment or a trial. Under which Peter Rugg now labors, I cannot say; therefore I am rather inclined to pity than to judge."

"You speak like a humane man," said I; "and if you have known him so long, I pray you will give me some account of him. Has his appearance much altered in that time?"

"Why, yes. He looks as though he never ate, drank or slept; and his child looks older than himself, and he looks like time broken off from eternity, and anxious to gain a resting-place."

"And how does his horse look?" said I.

"As for his horse, he looks fatter and gayer, and shows more animation and courage than he did twenty years ago. The last time Rugg spoke to me he inquired how far it was to Boston. I told him just one hundred miles.

" 'Why,' said he, 'how can you deceive me so? It is cruel to mislead a traveler. I have lost my way—pray direct me the nearest way to Boston?'

"I repeated, it was one hundred miles.

" 'How can you say so?' said he; 'I was told last evening it was but fifty, and I have traveled all night.'

" 'But,' said I, 'you are now traveling from Boston. You must turn back.'

" 'Alas,' said he, 'it is all turn back! Boston shifts with the wind, and plays all around the compass. One man tells me it is to the east, another to the west; and the guideposts, too—they all point the wrong way.'

" 'But will you not stop and rest?' said I. 'You seem wet and weary.'

" 'Yes,' said he, 'it has been foul weather since I left home.'

" 'Stop, then, and refresh yourself.'

" 'I must not stop; I must reach home tonight, if possible; though I think you must be mistaken in the distance to Boston.'

"He then gave the reins to his horse, which he restrained with difficulty, and disappeared in a moment. A few days afterwards I met the man a little this side of Claremont, winding around the hills in Unity, at the rate, I believe, of twelve miles an hour."

"Is Peter Rugg his real name, or has he accidentally gained that name?"

"I know not, but presume he will not deny his name; you can ask him—for, see, he has turned his horse, and is passing this way."

In a moment a dark-colored, high-spirited horse approached, and would have passed without stopping, but I had resolved to speak to Peter Rugg, or whoever the man might be. Accordingly, I stepped into the street; and as the horse approached, I made a feint of stopping him. The man immediately reined in his horse. "Sir," said I, "may I be so bold as to inquire if you are not Mr. Rugg? for I think I have seen you before."

"My name is Peter Rugg," said he. "I have unfortunately lost my way; I am wet and weary, and will take it kindly of you to direct me to Boston."

"You live in Boston, do you; and in what street?"

"In Middle Street."

"When did you leave Boston?"

"I cannot tell, precisely; it seems a considerable time."

"But how did you and your child become so wet? It has not rained here today."

"It has just rained a heavy shower up the river. But I shall not reach Boston tonight if I tarry. Would you advise me to take the old road or the turnpike?"

"Why, the old road is one hundred and seventeen miles, and the turnpike is ninety-seven."

"How can you say so? You impose on me; it is wrong to trifle with a traveler; you know it is but forty miles from Newburyport to Boston."

"But this is not Newburyport; this is Hartford."

"Do not deceive me, sir. Is not this town Newburyport, and the river that I have been following the Merrimac?"

"No, sir; this is Hartford, and the river the Connecticut."

He wrung his hands and looked incredulous. "Have the rivers, too, changed their courses, as the cities have changed places? But see! the clouds are gathering in the south, and we shall have a rainy night. Ah! that fatal oath!"

He would tarry no longer; his impatient horse leaped off, his hind flanks rising like wings; he seemed to devour all before him, and to scorn all behind.

I had now, as I thought, discovered a clue to the history of Peter Rugg; and I determined, the next time my business called me to Boston, to make a further inquiry. Soon after, I was enabled to collect the following particulars from Mrs. Croft, an aged lady in Middle Street, who has resided in Boston during the last twenty years. Her narration is this:

Just at twilight last summer a person stopped at the door of the late Mrs. Rugg. Mrs. Croft on coming to the door perceived a stranger with a child by his side, in an old weather-beaten carriage, with a black horse. The stranger asked for Mrs. Rugg, and was informed that Mrs. Rugg had died at a good old age, more than twenty years before that time.

The stranger replied, "How can you deceive me so? Do ask Mrs. Rugg to step to the door."

"Sir, I assure you Mrs. Rugg has not lived here these twenty years; no one lives here but myself, and my name is Betsey Croft."

The stranger paused, looked up and down the street, and said, "Though the paint is rather faded, this looks like my house."

"Yes," said the child, "that is the stone before the door that I used to sit on to eat my bread and milk."

"But," said the stranger, "it seems to be on the wrong side of the street. Indeed, everything here seems to be misplaced. The streets are all changed, the town seems changed, and what is strangest of all, Catherine Rugg has deserted her husband and child. Pray," continued the stranger, "has John Foy come home from sea? He went a long voyage; he is my kinsman. If I could see him, he could give me some account of Mrs. Rugg."

"Sir," said Mrs. Croft, "I never heard of John Foy. Where did he live?"

"Just above here, in Orange-tree Lane."

"There is no such place in this neighborhood."

"What do you tell me! Are the streets gone? Orange-tree Lane is at the head of Hanover Street, near Pemberton's Hill."

"There is no such lane now."

"Madam, you cannot be serious! But you doubtless know my brother, William Rugg. He lives in Royal Exchange Lane, near King Street."

"I know of no such lane; and I am sure there is no such street as King Street in this town."

"No such street as King Street! Why, woman, you mock me! You may as well tell me there is no King George. However, madam, you see I am wet and weary. I must find a resting-place. I will go to Hart's tavern, near the market."

"Which market, sir? for you seem perplexed. We have several markets."

"You know there is but one market near the town dock."

"Oh, the old market; but no such person has kept there these twenty years."

Here the stranger seemed disconcerted, and uttered to himself quite audibly, "Strange mistake; how much this looks like the town of Boston! It certainly has a great resemblance to it; but I perceive my mistake now. Some other Mrs. Rugg, some other Middle Street. Then," said he, "madam, can you direct me to Boston?"

"Why, this is Boston, the city of Boston; I know of no other Boston."

"City of Boston it may be; but it is not the Boston where I live. I recollect now, I came over a bridge instead of a ferry. Pray, what bridge is that I just came over?"

"It is Charles River Bridge."

"I perceive my mistake; there is a ferry between Boston and Charlestown; there is no bridge. Ah, I perceive my mistake. If I were in Boston my horse would carry me directly to my own door. But my horse shows by his impatience that he is in a strange place. Absurd, that I should have mistaken this place for the old town of Boston! It is a much finer city than the town of Boston. It has been built long since Boston. I fancy Boston must lie at a distance from this city, as the good woman seems ignorant of it."

At these words his horse began to chafe, and strike the

pavement with his forefeet. The stranger seemed a little bewildered, and said, "No home tonight"; and giving the reins to his horse passed up the street, and she saw no more of him.

It was evident that the generation to which Peter Rugg belonged had passed away.

This was all the account of Peter Rugg I could obtain from Mrs. Croft; but she directed me to an elderly man, Mr. James Felt, who lived near her, and who had kept a record of the principal occurrences for the last fifty years. At my request she sent for him; and after I had related to him the object of my inquiry, Mr. Felt told me he had known Rugg in his youth, and that his disappearance had caused some surprise; but as it sometimes happens that men run away—sometimes to be rid of others, and sometimes to be rid of themselves—and Rugg took his child with him, and his own horse and chair, and as it did not appear that any creditors made a stir, the occurrence soon mingled itself in the stream of oblivion; and Rugg and his child, horse and chair were soon forgotten.

"It is true," said Mr. Felt, "sundry stories grew out of Rugg's affair, whether true or false I cannot tell; but stranger things have happened in my day, without even a newspaper notice."

"Sir," said I, "Peter Rugg is now living. I have lately seen Peter Rugg and his child, horse and chair; therefore I pray you to relate to me all you know or ever heard of him."

"Why, my friend," said James Felt, "that Peter Rugg is

now a living man I will not deny; but that you have seen Peter Rugg and his child is impossible, if you mean a small child; for Jenny Rugg, if living, must be at least—let me see—Boston massacre, 1770—Jenny Rugg was about ten years old. Why, sir, Jenny Rugg, if living, must be more than sixty years of age. That Peter Rugg is living is highly probable, as he was only ten years older than myself, and I was only eighty last March; and I am as likely to live twenty years longer as any man."

Here I perceived that Mr. Felt was in his dotage, and I despaired of gaining any intelligence from him on which I could depend.

I took my leave of Mrs. Croft, and proceeded to my lodgings at the Marlborough Hotel.

"If Peter Rugg," thought I, "has been traveling since the Boston massacre, there is no reason why he should not travel to the end of time. If the present generation know little of him, the next will know less, and Peter and his child will have no hold on this world."

In the course of the evening I related my adventure in Middle Street.

"Ha!" said one of the company, smiling, "do you really think you have seen Peter Rugg? I have heard my grandfather speak of him as though he seriously believed his own story."

"Sir," said I, "pray let us compare your grandfather's story of Mr. Rugg with my own."

"Peter Rugg, sir—if my grandfather was worthy of

credit—once lived in Middle Street, in this city. He was a
man in comfortable circumstances, had a wife and one
daughter, and was generally esteemed for his sober life and
manners. But unhappily, his temper, at times, was altogether ungovernable, and then his language was terrible. In
these fits of passion, if a door stood in his way, he would
never do less than kick a panel through. He would sometimes throw his heels over his head, and come down on his
feet, uttering oaths in a circle; and thus in a rage, he was the
first who performed a somersault, and did what others have
since learned to do for merriment and money. Once Rugg
was seen to bite a tenpenny nail in halves. In those days
everybody, both men and boys, wore wigs; and Peter, at
these moments of violent passion, would become so profane
that his wig would rise up from his head. Some said it was on
account of his terrible language; others accounted for it in
a more philosophical way, and said it was caused by the
expansion of his scalp, as violent passion, we know, will
swell the veins and expand the head. While these fits were
on him, Rugg had no respect for heaven or earth. Except
for this infirmity, all agreed that Rugg was a good sort of a
man; for when his fits were over, nobody was so ready to
commend a placid temper as Peter.

"One morning, late in autumn, Rugg, in his own chair,
with a fine large bay horse, took his daughter and proceeded
to Concord. On his return a violent storm overtook him. At
dark he stopped in Menotomy, now West Cambridge, at the
door of a Mr. Cutter, a friend of his, who urged him to tarry

the night. On Rugg's declining to stop, Mr. Cutter urged him vehemently. 'Why, Mr. Rugg,' said Cutter, 'the storm is overwhelming you. The night is exceedingly dark. Your little daughter will perish. You are in an open chair, and the tempest is increasing.'

" '*Let the storm increase*,' said Rugg, with a fearful oath, '*I will see home tonight, in spite of the last tempest, or may I never see home!*' At these words he gave his whip to his high-spirited horse and disappeared in a moment. But Peter Rugg did not reach home that night, nor the next; nor, when he became a missing man, could he ever be traced beyond Mr. Cutter's, in Menotomy.

"For a long time after, on every dark and stormy night the wife of Peter Rugg would fancy she heard the crack of a whip, and the fleet tread of a horse, and the rattling of a carriage passing her door. The neighbors, too, heard the same noises, and some said they knew it was Rugg's horse; the tread on the pavement was perfectly familiar to them. This occurred so repeatedly that at length the neighbors watched with lanterns, and saw the real Peter Rugg, with his own horse and chair and the child sitting beside him, pass directly before his own door, his head turned toward his house, and himself making every effort to stop his horse, but in vain.

"The next day the friends of Mrs. Rugg exerted themselves to find her husband and child. They inquired at every public house and stable in town; but it did not appear that Rugg made any stay in Boston. No one, after Rugg had passed his own door, could give any account of him, though it was asserted by some that the clatter of Rugg's horse and carriage over the pavements shook the houses on both sides of the streets. And this is credible, if indeed Rugg's horse and carriage did pass on that night; for today, in many of the streets, a loaded truck or team in passing will shake the houses like an earthquake. However, Rugg's neighbors never afterward watched. Some of them treated it all as a delusion, and thought no more of it. Others of a different opinion shook their heads and said nothing.

"Thus Rugg and his child, horse, and chair were soon forgotten; and probably many in the neighborhood never heard a word on the subject.

"There was indeed a rumor that Rugg was seen afterward in Connecticut, between Suffield and Hartford, passing through the country at headlong speed. This gave occasion to Rugg's friends to make further inquiry; but the more they inquired, the more they were baffled. If they heard of Rugg one day in Connecticut, the next day they heard of him winding round the hills in New Hampshire; and soon after a man in a chair, with a small child, exactly answering the description of Peter Rugg, would be seen in Rhode Island inquiring the way to Boston.

"But that which gave a color of mystery to the story of Peter Rugg was the affair at Charlestown bridge. The toll-gatherer asserted that sometimes, on the darkest and most stormy nights, when no object could be discerned, about the time Rugg was missing, a horse and wheel-carriage, with a noise equal to a troop, would at midnight, in utter contempt of the rates of toll, pass over the bridge. This occurred so frequently that the toll-gatherer resolved to attempt a discovery. Soon after, at the usual time, apparently the same horse and carriage approached the bridge from Charlestown square. The toll-gatherer, prepared, took his stand as near the middle of the bridge as he dared, with a large three-legged stool in his hand. As the appearance passed, he threw the stool at the horse, but heard nothing except the noise of the stool skipping across the bridge. The toll-gatherer on the next day asserted that the stool went directly through the body of the horse, and he persisted in that belief ever after. Whether Rugg, or whoever the person was, ever passed the bridge again the toll-gatherer would never tell; and when questioned, he seemed anxious to waive the subject. And thus Peter Rugg and his child, horse and carriage remain a mystery to this day."

This, sir, is all that I could learn of Peter Rugg in Boston.

THE DEVIL
IN THE BELFRY
by Edgar Allan Poe

The fellow had, in spite of his grinning, an audacious and sinister kind of face.

Seven

What o'clock is it?—Old saying

EVERYBODY knows, in a general way, that the finest place in the world is—or, alas, *was*—the Dutch borough of Vondervotteimittiss. Yet, as it lies some distance from any of the main roads, being in a somewhat out-of-the-way situation, there are, perhaps, very few of my readers who have ever paid it a visit. For the benefit of those who have *not,* therefore, it will be only proper that I should enter into some account of it. And this is, indeed, the more necessary, as with the hope of enlisting public sentiment in behalf of the inhabitants, I design here to give a history of the calamitous events which have so lately occurred within its limits. No one who knows me will doubt that the duty thus self-imposed will be executed to the best of my ability, with all that rigid impartiality, all that cautious examination into facts, and diligent collation of authorities, which should ever distinguish him who aspires to the title of historian.

By the united aids of medals, manuscripts, and inscriptions, I am enabled to say, positively, that the borough of Vondervotteimittiss has existed, from its origin, in precisely the same condition which it at present preserves. . . . The oldest man in the borough can remember not the slightest difference in the appearance of any portion of it; and, indeed, the very suggestion of such a possibility is considered an insult. The site of the village is in a perfectly circular valley, about a quarter of a mile in circumference, and entirely surrounded by gentle hills over whose summit the people have never yet ventured to pass. For this they assign the very good reason that they do not believe there is anything at all on the other side.

Round the skirts of the valley (which is quite level, and paved throughout with flat tiles), extends a continuous row of sixty little houses. These, having their backs on the hills, must look, of course, to the center of the plain, which is just sixty yards from the front door of each dwelling. Every house has a small garden before it, with a circular path, a sun-dial, and twenty-four cabbages. The buildings themselves are so precisely alike that one can in no manner be distinguished from the other. Owing to the vast antiquity, the style of architecture is somewhat odd, but it is not for that reason the less strikingly picturesque. They are fashioned of hard-burned little bricks, red, with black ends, so that the walls look like a chessboard upon a great scale. The gables are turned to the front, and there are cornices, as big as all the rest of the house, over the eaves and over the main doors. The windows are narrow and deep, with very tiny panes and a great deal of sash. On the roof is a vast quantity of tiles with long curly ears. The woodwork, throughout, is of a dark hue, and there is much carving about it, with but a trifling variety of pattern; for, time out of mind, the carvers of Vondervotteimittiss have never been able to carve more than two objects—a timepiece and a cabbage. But these they do exceedingly well, and intersperse them, with singular ingenuity, wherever they find room for the chisel.

The dwellings are as much alike inside as out, and the furniture is all upon one plan. The floors are of square tiles, the chairs and tables of black-looking wood with thin crooked legs and puppy feet. The mantelpieces are wide and high, and have not only timepieces and cabbages sculptured over the front, but a real timepiece, which makes a prodigious ticking, on the top in the middle, with a flower-pot containing a cabbage standing on each extremity by way of outrider. Between each cabbage and the timepiece again, is a little china man having a large stomach with a great round hole in it, through which is seen the dial-plate of a watch.

The fireplaces are large and deep, with fierce crooked-looking fire-dogs. There is constantly a rousing fire, and a huge pot over it full of sauerkraut and pork, to which the good woman of the house is always busy in attending. She is a little fat old lady, with blue eyes and a red face, and wears a huge cap like a sugar-loaf, ornamented with purple and yellow ribbons. Her dress is of orange-colored linsey-woolsey made very full behind and very short in the waist—and indeed very short in other respects, not reaching below the middle of her leg. This is somewhat thick, and so are her ankles, but she has a fine pair of green stockings to cover them. Her shoes, of pink leather, are fastened each with a bunch of yellow ribbons puckered up in the shape of a cabbage. In her left hand she has a little heavy Dutch watch; in her right she wields a ladle for the sauerkraut and pork. By her side there stands a fat tabby cat, with a gilt toy repeater tied to its tail, which "the boys" have there fastened by way of a quiz.

The boys themselves are, all three of them, in the garden attending the pig. They are each two feet in height. They have three-cornered cocked hats, purple waistcoats reaching down to their thighs, buckskin knee-breeches, red woollen stockings, heavy shoes with big silver buckles, and long surtout coats with large buttons of mother-of-pearl. Each, too, has a pipe in his mouth, and a little dumpy watch in his right hand. He takes a puff and a look, and then a look and a puff. The pig, which is corpulent and lazy, is occupied now in picking up the stray leaves that fall from the cabbages, and now in giving a kick behind at the gilt repeater, which the urchins have also tied to *his* tail in order to make him look as handsome as the cat.

Right at the front door, in a high-backed leather-bottomed armed chair, with crooked legs and puppy feet like the tables, is seated the old man of the house himself. He is an exceedingly puffy little old gentleman, with big circular eyes and a huge double chin. His dress resembles that of the boys, and I need say nothing further about it. All the difference is that his pipe is somewhat bigger than theirs, and he can make a greater smoke. Like them, he has a watch, but he carries his watch in his pocket. To say the truth, he has something of more importance than a watch to attend to, and what that is I shall presently explain. He sits with his right leg upon his left knee, wears a grave countenance, and always keeps one of his eyes, at least, resolutely bent upon a certain remarkable object in the center of the plain.

This object is situated in the steeple of the House of the Town-Council. The Town-Council are all very little, round, oily, intelligent men, with big saucer eyes and fat double chins, and have their coats much longer and their shoe-buckles much bigger than the ordinary inhabitants of Von-dervotteimittiss. Since my sojourn in the borough they have had several special meetings, and have adopted these three important resolutions:

"That it is wrong to alter the good old course of things——"

"That there is nothing tolerable out of Vondervotteimit-tiss——" and

"That we will stick by our clocks and our cabbages."

Above the session-room of the Council is the steeple, and in the steeple is the belfry, where exists, and has existed time out of mind, the pride and wonder of the village—the great clock of the borough of Vondervotteimittiss. And this is the object to which the eyes of the old gentlemen are turned who sit in the leather-bottomed armchairs.

The great clock has seven faces—one in each of the seven sides of the steeple—so that it can be readily seen from all quarters. Its faces are large and white, and its hands heavy and black. There is a belfry-man whose sole duty is to attend to it; but this duty is the most perfect of sinecures—for the clock of Vondervotteimittiss was never yet known to have anything the matter with it. Until lately, the bare supposition of such a thing was considered heretical. From the remotest period of antiquity to which the archives have reference, the hours have been regularly struck by the big bell. And, indeed, the case was just the same with all the other clocks and watches in the borough. Never was such a place for keeping the true time. When the large clapper thought proper to say "Twelve o'clock!" all its obedient followers opened their throats simultaneously, and responded like a very echo. In short, the good burghers were fond of their sauerkraut, but then they were proud of their clocks.

All people who hold sinecure offices are held in more or less respect, and as the belfry-man of Vondervotteimittiss has the most perfect of sinecures, he is the most perfectly respected of any man in the world. He is the chief dignitary of the borough, and the very pigs look up to him with a sentiment of reverence. His coattail is *very* far longer—his pipe, his shoe buckles, his eyes, and his stomach, *very* far bigger—than those of any other old gentleman in the village; and as to his chin, it is not only double, but triple.

I have thus painted the happy estate of Vondervotteimit-tiss: alas, that so fair a picture should ever experience a reverse.

There has been long a saying among the wisest inhabi-tants, that "no good can come from over the hills"; and it really seemed that the words had in them something of the spirit of prophecy. It wanted five minutes of noon, on the day before yesterday, when there appeared a very odd-look-ing object on the summit of the ridge to the eastward. Such an occurrence, of course, attracted universal attention, and every little old gentleman who sat in a leather-bottomed armchair turned one of his eyes with a stare of dismay upon the phenomenon, still keeping the other upon the clock in the steeple.

By the time that it wanted only three minutes to noon, the droll object in question was perceived to be a very diminu-tive foreign-looking young man. He descended the hills at a great rate, so that everybody had soon a good look at him. He was really the most finicky little personage that had ever been seen in Vondervotteimittiss. His countenance was of a dark snuff-color, and he had a long hooked nose, pea eyes, a wide mouth, and an excellent set of teeth, which latter he seemed anxious of displaying, as he was grinning from ear to ear. What with mustachios and whiskers, there was none of the rest of his face to be seen. His head was uncovered, and his hair neatly done up on *papillotes*. His dress was a tight-fitting swallow-tailed black coat (from one of whose pockets dangled a vast length of white handkerchief), black kerseymere knee-breeches, black stockings, and stumpy-looking pumps, with huge bunches of black satin ribbon for bows. Under one arm he carried a huge *chapeau-de-bras,* and under the other a fiddle nearly five times as big as himself. In his left hand was a bold snuff-box, from which, as he capered down the hill, cutting all manner of fantastic steps, he took snuff incessantly with an air of the greatest possible self-satisfaction. God bless me!—here was a sight for the honest burghers of Vondervotteimittiss!

To speak plainly, the fellow had, in spite of his grinning, an audacious and sinister kind of face; and as he curveted right into the village, the odd stumpy appearance of his pumps excited no little suspicion; and many a burgher who beheld him that day would have given a trifle for a peep beneath the white cambric handkerchief which hung so obtrusively from the pocket of his swallow-tailed coat. But what mainly occasioned a righteous indignation was that the scoundrelly popinjay, while he cut a fandango here and a whirligig there, did not seem to have the remotest idea in the world of such a thing as *keeping time* in his steps.

The good people of the borough had scarcely a chance, however, to get their eyes thoroughly open, when just as it wanted half a minute of noon, the rascal bounced, as I say, right into the midst of them; gave a *chassez* here, and a *balancez* there; and then, after a *pirouette* and a *pas-de-zephyr,* pigeon-winged himself right up into the belfry of the House of the Town-Council, where the wonder-stricken belfry-man sat smoking in a state of dignity and dismay. But the little chap seized him at once by the nose; gave it a swing and a pull; clapped the big *chapeau-de-bras* upon his head; knocked it down over his eyes and mouth; and then, lifting up the big fiddle, beat him with it so long and so soundly that, what with the belfry-man being so fat and the fiddle being so hollow, you would have sworn that there was a regiment of double-bass drummers all beating the devil's tattoo up in the belfry of the steeple of Vondervotteimittiss.

There is no knowing to what desperate act of vengeance this unprincipled attack might have aroused the inhabitants, but for the important fact that it now wanted only half a second of noon. The bell was about to strike, and it was a matter of absolute and pre-eminent necessity that everybody should look well at his watch. It was evident, however, that just at this moment the fellow in the steeple was doing something that he had no business to do with the clock. But as it now began to strike, nobody had any time to attend to his maneuvers, for they had all to count the strokes of the bell as it sounded.

"One!" said the clock.

"Von!" echoed every little old gentleman in every leather-bottomed armchair in Vondervotteimittiss. "Von!" said his watch also; "von!" said the watch of his vrow; and "von!" said the watches of the boys, and the little gilt repeaters on the tails of the cat and pig.

"Two!" continued the big bell; and

"Doo!" repeated all the repeaters.

"Three! Four! Five! Six! Seven! Eight! Nine! Ten!" said the bell.

"Dree! Vour! Fibe! Sax! Seben! Aight! Noin! Den!" answered the others.

"Eleven!" said the big one.

"Eleben!" assented the little ones.

"Twelve!" said the bell.

"Dvelf!" they replied, perfectly satisfied, and dropping their voices.

"Und dvelf it iss!" said all the little old gentlemen, putting up their watches. But the big bell had not done with them yet.

"*Thirteen!*" said he.

"Der Teufel!" gasped the little old gentlemen, turning pale, dropping their pipes, and putting down all their right legs from over their left knees.

"Der Teufel!" groaned they. "Dirteen! Dirteen!!—Mein Gott, it is dirteen o'clock!!"

Why attempt to describe the terrible scene which ensued? All Vondervotteimittiss flew at once into a lamentable state of uproar.

"Vot is cum'd to mein pelly?" roared all the boys—"I've been ongry for dis hour!"

"Vot is cum'd to mein kraut?" screamed all the vrows. "It has been done to rags for dis hour!"

"Vot is cum'd to mein pipe?" swore all the little old gentlemen. "Donder and Blitzen! it has been smoked out for dis hour!"—and they filled them up again in a great rage, and, sinking back in their armchairs, puffed away so fast and so fiercely that the whole valley was immediately filled with impenetrable smoke.

Meantime the cabbages all turned very red in the face, and it seemed as if old Nick himself had taken possession of everything in the shape of a timepiece. The clocks carved upon the furniture took to dancing as if bewitched, while those upon the mantelpieces could scarcely contain themselves for fury, and kept such a continual striking of thirteen, and such a frisking and wriggling of their pendulums as was really horrible to see. But worse than all, neither the cats nor the pigs could put up any longer with the behavior of the little repeaters tied to their tails, and resented it by scampering all over the place, scratching and poking, and squeaking and screeching, and caterwauling and squalling, and flying into the faces, and running under the petticoats of the people, and creating altogether the most abominable din and confusion which it is possible for a reasonable person to conceive. And to make matters still more distressing, the rascally little scapegrace in the steeple was evidently exerting himself to the utmost. Every now and then one might catch a glimpse of the scoundrel through the smoke. There he sat in the belfry upon the belfry-man, who was lying flat upon his back. In his teeth the villain held the bell-rope, which he kept jerking about with his head, raising such a clatter that my ears ring again even to think of it. On his lap lay the big fiddle, at which he was scraping, out of all time and tune, with both hands, making a great show, the nincompoop! of playing "Judy O'Flannagan and Paddy O'Rafferty."

Affairs being thus miserably situated, I left the place in disgust, and now appeal for aid to all lovers of correct time and fine kraut. Let us proceed in a body to the borough, and restore the ancient order of things in Vondervotteimittiss by ejecting that little fellow from the steeple.

THE SPECTRE
BRIDEGROOM

by Washington Irving

He was a gallant cavalier, mounted on a black steed.

Eight

O N the summit of one of the heights of the Odenwald, a wild and romantic tract of Upper Germany that lies not far from the confluence of the Maine and the Rhine, there stood, many, many years since, the Castle of the Baron Von Landshort. It was now quite fallen to decay, and almost buried among beech trees and dark firs; above which, however, its old watch-tower may still be seen struggling, like the former possessor I have mentioned, to carry a high head, and look down upon a neighboring country.

The Baron was a dry branch of the great family of Katzenellenbogen, and inherited the relics of the property, and all the pride of his ancestors. Though the warlike disposition of his predecessors had much impaired the family possessions, yet the Baron still endeavored to keep up some show of former state. The times were peaceable, and the German nobles, in general, had abandoned their inconvenient old castles, perched like eagles' nests among the mountains, and had built more convenient residences in the valleys; still the Baron remained proudly drawn up in his fortress, cherishing with hereditary inveteracy all the old family feuds; so that he was on ill terms with some of his nearest neighbors, on account of disputes that had happened between their great-great-grandfathers.

The Baron had but one child, a daughter; but Nature, when she grants but one child, always compensates by making it a prodigy; and so it was with the daughter of the Baron. All the nurses, gossips, and country cousins assured her father that she had not her equal for beauty in all Germany; and who should know better than they? She had, moreover, been brought up with great care, under the superintendence of two maiden aunts, who had spent some years of their early life at one of the little German courts, and were skilled in all the branches of knowledge necessary to the education of a fine lady. Under their instructions, she became a miracle of accomplishments. By the time she was eighteen she could embroider to admiration, and had worked whole histories of the saints in tapestry, with such strength of expression in their countenances, that they looked like so many souls in purgatory. She could read without great difficulty, and had spelled her way through several church legends, and almost all the chivalric wonders of the Heldenbuch. She had even made considerable proficiency in writing, could sign her own name without missing a letter, and so legibly that her aunts could read it without spectacles. She excelled in making little good-for-nothing ladylike knickknacks of all kinds; was versed in the most abstruse dancing of the day; played a number of airs on the harp and guitar; and knew all the tender ballads of the Minnie-lieders by heart.

Her aunts, too, having been great flirts and coquettes in their younger days, were admirably calculated to be vigilant guardians and strict censors of the conduct of their niece; for there is no duenna so rigidly prudent and inexorably decorous as a superannuated coquette. She was rarely suffered out of their sight; never went beyond the domains of the castle, unless well attended, or rather well watched; had continual lectures read to her about strict decorum and implicit obedience; and, as to the men—pah! she was taught to hold them at such distance and distrust, that, unless properly authorized, she would not have cast a glance upon the handsomest cavalier in the world—no, not if he were even dying at her feet.

The good effects of this system were wonderfully apparent. The young lady was a pattern of docility and correctness. While others were wasting their sweetness in the glare of the world, she was coyly blooming into fresh and lovely womanhood under the protection of those immaculate spinsters, like a rosebud blushing forth among guardian thorns. Her aunts looked upon her with pride and exultation.

But however scantily the Baron Von Landshort might be provided with children, his household was by no means a small one, for Providence had enriched him with an abundance of poor relations. They, one and all, possessed the affectionate disposition common to humble relatives; were wonderfully attached to the Baron, and took every possible occasion to come in swarms and enliven the castle. All family festivals were commemorated by these good people at the Baron's expense; and when they were filled with good cheer, they would declare that there was nothing on earth so delightful as these family meetings, these jubilees of the heart.

The Baron, though a small man, had a large soul, and it swelled with satisfaction at the consciousness of being the greatest man in the little world about him. He loved to tell long stories about the stark old warriors whose portraits looked grimly down from the walls around, and he found no listeners equal to those who fed at his expense. He was much given to the marvelous and a firm believer in all those supernatural tales with which every mountain and valley in Germany abounds. The faith of his guests even exceeded his own: they listened to every tale of wonder with open eyes and mouth, and never failed to be astonished, even though repeated for the hundredth time. Thus lived the Baron Von Landshort, the oracle of his table, the absolute monarch of his little territory, and happy, above all things, in the persuasion that he was the wisest man of the age.

At the time of which my story treats, there was a great family-gathering at the castle, on an affair of the utmost importance: it was to receive the destined bridegroom of the Baron's daughter. A negotiation had been carried on between the father and an old nobleman of Bavaria, to unite the dignity of their houses by the marriage of their children. The preliminaries had been conducted with proper punctilio. The young people were betrothed without seeing each other, and the time was appointed for the marriage ceremony. The young Count Von Altenburg had been recalled from the army for the purpose, and was actually on his way to the Baron's to receive his bride. Missives had even been received from him, from Würtzburg, mentioning the day and hour when he might be expected to arrive.

The castle was in a tumult of preparation to give him a suitable welcome. The fair bride had been decked out with uncommon care. The two aunts had superintended her toilet, and quarreled the whole morning about every article of her dress. The young lady had taken advantage of their contest to follow the bent of her own taste; and fortunately it was a good one. She looked as lovely as a youthful bridegroom could desire; and the flutter of expectation heightened the lustre of her charms.

The suffusions that mantled her face and neck, the gentle heaving of the bosom, the eye now and then lost in reverie, all betrayed the soft tumult that was going on in her little heart.

The Baron was no less busied in preparations. He had, in truth, nothing exactly to do; but he was naturally a fuming, bustling little man, and could not remain passive when all the world was in a hurry. He worried from top to bottom of the castle with an air of infinite anxiety; he continually called the servants from their work to exhort them to be diligent, and buzzed about every hall and chamber, as idly restless and importunate as a blue-bottle fly on a warm summer's day.

In the meantime, the fatted calf had been killed; the forests had rung with the clamor of the huntsmen; the kitchen was crowded with good cheer; the cellars had yielded up whole oceans of *Rhein-wein* and *Ferne-wein,* and even the great Heidelburg tun had been laid under contribution. Everything was ready to receive the distinguished guest in the true spirit of German hospitality—but the guest delayed to make his appearance. Hour rolled after hour. The sun that had poured his downward rays upon the rich forests of the Odenwald now just gleamed along the summits of the mountains. The Baron mounted the highest tower, and strained his eyes in hope of catching a distant sight of the Count and his attendants. Once he thought he beheld them; the sound of horns came floating from the valley, prolonged by the mountain echoes: a number of horsemen were seen far below, slowly advancing along the road; but when they had nearly reached the foot of the mountain, they suddenly struck off in a different direction. The last ray of sunshine departed—the bats began to flit by in the twilight—the road grew dimmer and dimmer to the view; and nothing appeared stirring in it but now and then a peasant lagging homeward from his labor.

While the old castle of Landshort was in this state of perplexity, a very interesting scene was transacting in a different part of the Odenwald.

The young Count Von Altenburg was tranquilly pursuing his route in that sober jog-trot way in which a man travels towards matrimony when his friends have taken all the trouble and uncertainty of courtship off his hands, and a bride is waiting for him, as certainly as a dinner, at the end of his journey. He had encountered at Würtzburg a youthful companion in arms, with whom he had seen some service on the frontiers; Herman Von Starkenfaust, one of the stoutest hands and worthiest hearts of German chivalry, who was now returning from the army. His father's castle was not far distant from the old fortress of Landshort, although an hereditary feud rendered the families hostile, and strangers to each other.

In the warm-hearted moment of recognition, the young friends related all their past adventures and fortunes, and the Count gave the whole history of his intended nuptials with a young lady he had never seen, but of whose charms he had received the most enrapturing descriptions.

As the route of the friends lay in the same direction, they agreed to perform the rest of their journey together; and that they might do it more leisurely, set off from Würtzburg at an early hour, the Count having given directions for his retinue to follow and overtake him.

They beguiled their wayfaring with recollections of their military scenes and adventures; but the Count was apt to be a little tedious, now and then, about the reputed charms of his bride, and the felicity that awaited him.

In this way they had entered among the mountains of the Odenwald, and were traversing one of its most lonely and thickly wooded passes. It is well known that the forests of Germany have always been as much infested with robbers as its castles with spectres; and, at this time, the former were particularly numerous, from the hordes of disbanded soldiers wandering idly about the country. It will not appear extraordinary, therefore, that the cavaliers were attacked by a gang of these stragglers, in the midst of the forest. They defended themselves with bravery, but were nearly overpowered when the Count's retinue arrived to their assistance. At sight of them the robbers fled, but not until the Count had received a mortal wound. He was slowly and carefully conveyed back to the city of Würtzburg, and a friar summoned from a neighboring convent, who was famous for his skill in administering to both soul and body. But half of his skill was superfluous; the moments of the unfortunate Count were numbered.

With his dying breath he entreated his friend to repair instantly to the castle of Landshort, and explain the fatal cause of his not keeping his appointment with his bride. Though not the most ardent of lovers, he was one of the most punctilious of men, and appeared earnestly solicitous that this mission should be speedily and courteously executed. "Unless this is done," said he, "I shall not sleep quietly in my grave!" He repeated these last words with peculiar solemnity. A request, at a moment so impressive, admitted no hesitation. Starkenfaust endeavored to soothe him to calmness; promised faithfully to execute his wish, and gave him his hand in solemn pledge. The dying man pressed it in acknowledgment, but soon lapsed into delirium —raved about his bride—his engagements—his plighted word; ordered his horse, that he might ride to the castle of Landshort, and expired in the fancied act of vaulting into the saddle.

Starkenfaust bestowed a sigh and a soldier's tear on the untimely fate of his comrade, and then pondered on the awkward mission he had undertaken. His heart was heavy and his head perplexed; for he was to present himself an unbidden guest among hostile people, and to damp their festivity with tidings fatal to their hopes. Still there were certain whisperings of curiosity in his bosom to see this far-famed beauty of Katzenellenbogen, so cautiously shut up from the world.

Previous to his capture, he made all due arrangements with the holy fraternity of the convent for the funeral solemnities of his friend, who was to be buried in the cathedral of Würtzburg, near some of his illustrious relatives; and the mourning retinue of the Count took charge of his remains.

It is now high time that we should return to the ancient family of Katzenellenbogen, who were impatient for their guest, and still more for their dinner; and to the worthy little Baron, whom we left airing himself on the watch-tower.

Night closed in, but still no guest arrived. The Baron descended from the tower in despair. The banquet, which had been delayed from hour to hour, could no longer be postponed. The meats were already overdone; the cook in an agony; and the whole household had the look of a garrison that had been reduced by famine. The Baron was obliged reluctantly to give orders for the feast without the presence of the guest. All were seated at table, and just on the point of commencing, when the sound of a horn from without the gate gave notice of the approach of a stranger. Another long blast filled the old courts of the castle with its echoes, and was answered by the warder from the walls. The Baron hastened to receive his future son-in-law.

The drawbridge had been let down, and the stranger was before the gate. He was a tall, gallant cavalier, mounted on a black steed. His countenance was pale, but he had a beaming, romantic eye and an air of stately melancholy. The Baron was a little mortified that he should have come in this simple, solitary style. His dignity for a moment was ruffled, and he felt disposed to consider it a want of proper respect for the important occasion and the important family with which he was to be connected. He pacified himself, however, with the conclusion that it must have been youthful impatience which had induced him thus to spur on sooner than his attendants.

"I am sorry," said the stranger, "to break in upon you thus unseasonably——"

Here the Baron interrupted him with a world of compliments and greetings; for, to tell the truth, he prided himself upon his courtesy and his eloquence. The stranger attempted, once or twice, to stem the torrent of words, but in vain; so he bowed his head and suffered it to flow on. By the time the Baron had come to a pause, they had reached the inner court of the castle; and the stranger was again about to speak when he was once more interrupted by the appearance of the female part of the family, leading forth the shrinking and blushing bride. He gazed on her for a moment as one entranced; it seemed as if his whole soul beamed forth in the gaze and rested upon that lovely form. One of the maiden aunts whispered something in her ear; she made an effort to speak; her moist blue eye was timidly raised, gave a shy glance of inquiry on the stranger, and was cast again to the ground. The words died away; but there was a sweet smile playing about her lips, and a soft dimpling of the cheek, that showed her glance had not been unsatisfactory. It was impossible for a girl of the fond age of eighteen, highly predisposed for love and matrimony, not to be pleased with so gallant a cavalier.

The late hour at which the guest had arrived left no time for parley. The Baron was peremptory, and deferred all particular conversation until the morning, and led the way to the untasted banquet.

The cavalier took but little notice of the company or the entertainment. He scarcely tasted the banquet, but seemed absorbed in admiration of his bride. He conversed in a low tone that could not be overheard—for the language of love is never loud. There was a mingled tenderness and gravity in his manner that appeared to have a powerful effect upon the young lady. Her color came and went, as she listened with deep attention. Now and then she made some blushing reply, and when his eye was turned away, she would steal a sidelong glance at his romantic countenance and heave a gentle sigh of tender happiness. It was evident that the young couple were completely enamoured. The aunts, who were deeply versed in the mysteries of the heart, declared that they had fallen in love with each other at first sight.

The feast went on merrily, or at least noisily, for the guests were all blessed with those keen appetites that attend upon light purses and mountain air. The Baron told his best and longest stories, and never had he told them so well or with such great effect.

Amidst all this revelry, the stranger guest maintained a most singular and unseasonable gravity. His countenance assumed a deeper cast of dejection as the evening advanced, and, strange as it may appear, even the Baron's jokes seemed only to render him the more melancholy. At times he was lost in thought, and at times there was a perturbed and restless wandering of the eye that bespoke a mind but ill at ease. His conversations with the bride became more and more earnest and mysterious. Lowering clouds began to steal over the fair serenity of her brow, and tremors to run through her tender frame.

All this could not escape the notice of the company. Their gaiety was chilled by the unaccountable gloom of the bridegroom; their spirits were infected; whispers and glances were interchanged, accompanied by shrugs and dubious shakes of the head. The song and the laugh grew less frequent; there were dreary pauses in the conversation, which were at length succeeded by wild tales and supernatural legends. One dismal story produced another still more dismal, and the Baron nearly frightened some of the ladies into hysterics with the history of the goblin horseman that carried away the fair Leonora—a dreadful but true story, which has since been put into excellent verse and is read and believed by all the world.

The bridegroom listened to this tale with profound attention. He kept his eyes steadily fixed on the Baron, and as the story drew to a close, began gradually to rise from his seat, growing taller and taller, until, in the Baron's entranced eye, he seemed almost to tower into a giant. The moment the tale was finished, he heaved a deep sigh, and took a solemn farewell of the company. They were all amazement. The Baron was perfectly thunderstruck.

"What! going to leave the castle at midnight? why, everything was prepared for his reception; a chamber was ready for him if he wished to retire."

The stranger shook his head mournfully and mysteriously. "I must lay my head in a different chamber tonight!"

There was something in this reply and the tone in which it was uttered that made the Baron's heart misgive him, but he rallied his forces and repeated his hospitable entreaties. The stranger shook his head silently but positively at every offer, and waving his farewell to the company, stalked slowly out of the hall. The maiden aunts were absolutely petrified—the bride hung her head, and a tear stole to her eye.

The Baron followed the stranger to the great court of the castle, where the black charger stood pawing the earth and snorting with impatience. When they had reached the portal, whose deep archway was dimly lighted by a cresset, the stranger paused, and addressed the Baron in a hollow tone of voice, which the vaulted roof rendered still more sepulchral. "Now that we are alone," said he, "I will impart to you the reason of my going. I have a solemn, an indispensable engagement——"

"Why," said the Baron, "cannot you send some one in your place?"

"It admits of no substitute—I must attend it in person—I must away to Würtzburg cathedral——"

"Ay," said the Baron, plucking up spirit, "but not until tomorrow—tomorrow you shall take your bride there."

"No! no!" replied the stranger, with tenfold solemnity, "my engagement is with no bride—the worms! the worms expect me! I am a dead man—I have been slain by robbers—my body lies at Würtzburg—at midnight I am to be buried—the grave is waiting for me—I must keep my appointment!"

He sprang on his black charger, dashed over the drawbridge, and the clattering of his horse's hoofs was lost in the whistling of the night-blast.

The Baron returned to the hall in the utmost consterna-
tion and related what had passed. Two ladies fainted out-
right; others sickened at the idea of having banqueted with
a spectre. It was the opinion of some that this might be the
wild huntsman famous in German legend. Some talked of
mountain sprites, of wood-demons, and of other supernatural beings with which the good people of Germany
have been so grievously harassed since time immemorial.

But, whatever may have been the doubts entertained, they
were completely put to an end by the arrival, next day, of
regular missives, confirming the intelligence of the young
Count's murder, and his internment in Würtzburg cathedral.

The dismay at the castle may well be imagined. The
Baron shut himself up in his chamber. The guests who had
come to rejoice with him could not think of abandoning
him in his distress. They wandered about the courts, or col-
lected in groups in the hall, shaking their heads and shrug-
ging their shoulders at the troubles of so good a man; and
sat longer than ever at table, and ate and drank more stoutly
than ever, by way of keeping up their spirits. But the situation of the widowed bride was the most pitiable. To have
lost a husband before she had even embraced him—and
such a husband! if the very spectre could be so gracious and
noble what must have been the living man? She filled the
house with lamentations.

On the night of the second day of her widowhood, she
had retired to her chamber, accompanied by one of her

aunts, who insisted on sleeping with her. The aunt, who was one of the best tellers of ghost stories in all Germany, had just been recounting one of her longest, and had fallen asleep in the very midst of it. The chamber was remote, and overlooked a small garden. The niece lay pensively gazing at the beams of the rising moon, as they trembled on the leaves of an aspen tree before the lattice. The castle clock had just told midnight when a soft strain of music stole up from the garden. She rose hastily from her bed, and stepped lightly to the windows. A tall figure stood among the shadows of the trees. As it raised its head, a beam of moonlight fell upon the countenance. Heaven and earth! she beheld the Spectre Bridegroom! A loud shriek at that moment burst upon her ear, and her aunt, who had been awakened by the music, and had followed her silently to the window, fell into her arms. When she looked again, the spectre had disappeared.

Of the two females, the aunt now required the most soothing, for she was perfectly beside herself with terror. As to the young lady, there was something, even in the spectre of her lover, that seemed endearing. The aunt declared that she would never sleep in that chamber again; the niece, for once, was refractory, and declared as strongly that she would sleep in no other in the castle: the consequence was, that she had to sleep in it alone; but she drew a promise from her aunt not to relate the story of the spectre, lest she should be denied the only melancholy pleasure left her on earth—

that of inhabiting the chamber over which the guardian shade of her lover kept its nightly vigils.

How long the good old lady would have observed this promise is uncertain, for she dearly loved to talk of the marvelous, and there is a triumph in being the first to tell a frightful story; it is, however, still quoted in the neighborhood, as a memorable instance of female secrecy, that she kept it to herself for a whole week; when she was suddenly absolved from all restraint by intelligence brought to the breakfast-table one morning that the young lady was not to be found. Her room was empty—the bed had not been slept in—the window was open—and the bird had flown!

The astonishment and concern with which this intelligence was received can only be imagined by those who have witnessed the agitation which the mishaps of a great man cause among his friends. Even the poor relations paused for a moment from the indefatigable labors of the trencher when the aunt, who had at first been struck speechless, wrung her hands and shrieked out, "The goblin! the goblin! she's carried away by the goblin!"

In a few words she related the fearful scene of the garden, and concluded that the spectre must have carried off his bride. Two of the domestics corroborated the opinion, for they had heard the clattering of a horse's hoofs down the mountain about midnight, and had no doubt that it was the spectre on his black charger, bearing her away to the tomb. All present were struck with the direful probability; for events of the kind are extremely common in Germany, as many well-authenticated histories bear witness.

What a lamentable situation was that of the poor Baron! What a heart-rending dilemma for a fond father, and a member of the great family of Katzenellenbogen! His only daughter had either been rapt away to the grave, or he was to have some wood-demon for a son-in-law, and, perchance, a troop of goblin grandchildren. As usual, he was completely bewildered, and all the castle in an uproar. The men were ordered to take horse and scour every road and path and glen of the Odenwald. The Baron himself had just drawn on his jack-boots, girded on his sword, and was about to mount his steed to sally forth on the doubtful quest when he was brought to pause by a new apparition. A lady was seen approaching the castle, mounted on a palfrey attended by a cavalier on horseback. She galloped up to the gate, sprang from her horse, and falling at the Baron's feet, embraced his knees. It was his lost daughter, and her companion—the Spectre Bridegroom! The Baron was astounded. He looked at his daughter, then at the spectre, and almost doubted the evidence of his senses. The latter, too, was wonderfully improved in his appearance, since his visit to the world of spirits. His dress was splendid, and set off a noble figure of manly symmetry. He was no longer pale and melancholy. His fine countenance was flushed with the glow of youth, and joy rioted in his large dark eyes.

The mystery was soon cleared up. The cavalier (for in truth, as you must have known all the while, he was no

goblin) announced himself as Sir Herman Von Starkenfaust. He related his adventure with the young Count. He
told how he had hastened to the castle to deliver the un-
welcome tidings, but that the eloquence of the Baron had
interrupted him in every attempt to tell his tale. How the
sight of the bride had completely captivated him, and that
to pass a few hours, he had tacitly suffered the mistake to
continue. How he had been sorely perplexed in what way
to make a decent retreat, until the Baron's goblin stories
had suggested his eccentric exit. How, fearing the feudal
hostility of the family, he had repeated his visits by stealth
—had haunted the garden beneath the young lady's window—had wooed—had won—had borne away in triumph
—and, in a word, had wedded the fair.

Under any other circumstance, the Baron would have
been inflexible, for he was tenacious of paternal authority
and devoutly obstinate in all family feuds; but he loved his
daughter; he had lamented her as lost; he rejoiced to find
her still alive; and, though her husband was of a hostile
house, yet, thank Heaven, he was not a goblin.

Matters, therefore, were happily arranged. The Baron
pardoned the young couple on the spot. The revels at the
castle were resumed. The poor relations overwhelmed this
new member of the family with loving kindness; he was so
gallant, so generous—and so rich. The aunts, it is true, were
somewhat scandalized that their system of strict seclusion
and passive obedience should be so badly exemplified, but
attributed it all to their negligence in not having the win-

dows grated. One of them was particularly mortified at having her marvelous story marred, and that the only spectre she had ever seen should turn out a counterfeit; but the niece seemed perfectly happy at having found him substantial flesh and blood—and so the story ends.

HAUNTED SUBALTERNS

by Rudyard Kipling

*"Now we've got It!" said Horrocks as he threw the
door open, and let fly with the twelve-bore.*

⤙ *Nine*

So long as the "Inextinguishables" confined themselves to running picnics, gymkhanas, flirtations and innocences of that kind, no one said anything. But when they ran ghosts, people put up their eyebrows. 'Man can't feel comfy with a regiment that entertains ghosts on its establishment. It's against General Orders. The "Inextinguishables" said that the ghosts were private and not Regimental property. They referred you to Tesser for particulars; and Tesser told you to go to—the hottest cantonment of all. He said that it was bad enough to have men making hay of his bedding and breaking his banjo-strings when he was out, without being chaffed afterward; and he would thank you to keep your remarks on ghosts to yourself. This was before the "Inextinguishables" had sworn by their several lady-loves that they were innocent of any intrusion into Tesser's quarters. Then Horrocks mentioned casually at Mess that a couple of white figures had been bounding about his room the night before, and he didn't approve of it. The "Inextinguishables" denied, energetically, that they had had any hand in the manifestations, and advised Horrocks to consult Tesser.

I don't suppose that a Subaltern believes in anything except his chances of a Company; but Horrocks and Tesser were exceptions. They came to believe in their ghosts. They had reason.

Horrocks used to find himself at about three o'clock in the morning, staring wide-awake, watching two white things hopping about his room and jumping up to the ceiling. Horrocks was of a placid turn of mind. After a week or so spent in watching his servants, and lying in wait for strangers, and trying to keep awake all night, he came to the conclusion that he was haunted, and that, consequently, he need not bother. He wasn't going to encourage these ghosts by being frightened at them. Therefore when he awoke—as usual—with a start and saw these Things jumping like kangaroos, he only murmured, "Go on! Don't mind me!" and went to sleep again.

Tesser said, "It's all very well for you to make fun of your show. You can see your ghosts. Now, I can't see mine, and I don't half like it."

Tesser used to come into his room of nights and find the whole of his bedding neatly stripped, as if it had been done with one sweep of the hand, from the top right-hand corner of the charpoy to the bottom left-hand corner. Also his lamp used to lie weltering on the floor, and generally his pet

screw-head, inlaid, nickel-plated banjo was lying on the
charpoy, with all its strings broken. Tesser took away the
strings on the occasion of the third manifestation, and
the next night a man complimented him on his playing the
best music ever got out of a banjo for half an hour.

"Which half hour?" said Tesser.

"Between nine and ten," said the man. Tesser had gone
out to dinner at seven-thirty and had returned at midnight.

He talked to his bearer and threatened him with unspeakable things. The bearer was gray with fear. "I am a poor
man," said he. "If the Sahib is haunted by a devil, what can
I do?"

"Who says I am haunted by a devil" howled Tesser, for
he was angry.

"I have seen It," said the bearer, "at night, walking
round and round your bed; and that is why everything is
ulta-pulta in your room. I am a poor man, but I never go
into your room alone. The *bhisti* comes with me."

Tesser was thoroughly savage at this, and he spoke to Horrocks, and the two laid traps to catch the devil, and threatened their servants with dog-whips if any more *"Shaitan-ke-
hanky-panky"* took place. But the servants were soaked with
fear, and it was no use adding to their tortures. When Tesser
went out at night, four of his men, as a rule, slept in the
veranda of his quarters, until the banjo without the strings
struck up, and then they fled.

One time Tesser had to put in a month at the Fort with a
detachment of "Inextinguishables." The Fort might have

been Govindghar, Jumrood or Phillour; but it wasn't. He left cantonments rejoicing, for his devil was preying on his mind, and with him went another Subaltern, a junior. But the devil came too. After Tesser had been in the Fort about ten days he went out to dinner. When he came back he found his Subaltern doing sentry on the banquette across the Fort ditch, as far removed as might be from the Officers' quarters.

"What's wrong?" said Tesser.

The Subaltern said, "Listen!" and the two, standing under the stars, heard from the Officers' quarters, high up in the wall of the Fort, the *"strumty tumty tumty"* of the banjo; which seemed to have an oratorio on hand.

"That performance," said the Subaltern, "has been going on for three mortal hours. I never wished to desert before, but I do now. I say, Tesser, old man, you are the best of good fellows, I'm sure, but—I say—look here, now, you are quite unfit to live with. 'Tisn't in my Commission, you know, that I'm to serve under a—a—man with devils."

"Isn't it?" said Tesser. "If you make an ass of yourself, I'll put you under arrest—*and in my room!*"

"You can put me where you please, but I'm not going to assist at these infernal concerts. 'Tisn't right. 'Tisn't natural. Look here, I don't want to hurt your feelings, but—try to think now—haven't you done something—committed some—murder that has slipped your memory—or forged something——?"

"Well! For an all-round, double-shotted, half-baked fool you are the——"

"I dare say I am," said the Subaltern. "But you don't expect me to keep my wits with that row going on, do you?"

The banjo was rattling away as if it had twenty strings. Tesser sent up a stone, and a shower of broken windowpane fell into the Fort ditch; but the banjo kept on. Tesser hauled the other Subaltern up to the quarters, and found his room in frightful confusion—lamp upset, bedding all over the floor, chairs overturned and table tilted sideways. He took stock of the wreck, and said despairingly, "Oh, this is lovely!"

The Subaltern was peeping in at the door.

"I'm glad you think so," said he. " 'Tisn't lovely enough for me. I *locked* up your room directly after you had gone out. See here, I think you'd better apply for Horrocks to come out in my place. He's troubled with your complaint, and this business will make a jabbering idiot of me if it goes on."

Tesser went to bed amid the wreckage, very angry, and next morning he rode into cantonments and asked Horrocks to arrange to relieve "that fool with me now."

"You've got 'em again, have you?" said Horrocks. "So've I. *Three* white figures this time. We'll worry through it together."

So Horrocks and Tesser settled down in the Fort together, and the "Inextinguishables" said pleasant things about "seven other devils." Tesser didn't see where the joke came in. His room was thrown upside down three nights out of the seven. Horrocks was not troubled in any way, so his ghosts must have been purely local ones. Tesser, on the other hand, was personally haunted; for his devil had come with him from cantonments to the Fort. Those two boys spent three parts of their time trying to find out *who* was responsible for the riot in Tesser's rooms. At the end of a fortnight they tried to find out *what* was responsible; and seven days later they gave it up as a bad job.

Whatever It was, It refused to be caught; even when Tesser went out of the Fort ostentatiously and Horrocks lay under his charpoy with a revolver. The servants were afraid —more afraid than ever—and all the evidence showed that they had been playing no tricks. As Tesser said to Horrocks, "A haunted Subaltern is a joke, but s'pose this keeps on. Just think what a haunted Colonel would be. And, look here—s'pose I marry! D' you s'pose a girl would live a week with me *and* this devil?"

"I don't know," said Horrocks. "I haven't married often; but I knew a woman once who lived with her husband when he had delirium tremens. He's dead now, and I dare say *she* would marry you if you asked her. She isn't exactly a girl, though, but she has had a large experience of the *other* devils—the blue variety. She's a Government pensioner now, and you might write, y' know. Personally, if I hadn't suffered from ghosts of my own, I should rather avoid you."

"That's just the point," said Tesser. "This devil thing

will end in getting me *budnamed,* and you know I've lived on lemon-squashes and gone to bed at ten for weeks past."

" 'Tisn't that sort of devil," said Horrocks. "It's either a first-class fraud for which some one ought to be killed or else you've offended one of these Indian devils. It stands to reason that such a beastly country should be full of fiends of all sorts."

"But why should the creature fix on *me?*" said Tesser, "and why won't he show himself and have it out like a— like the Devil?"

They were talking outside the Mess after dark, and, even as they spoke, they heard the banjo begin to play in Tesser's room, about twenty yards off.

Horrocks ran to his own quarters for a shotgun and re- volver, and Tesser and he crept up quickly, the banjo still playing, to Tesser's door.

"Now we've got It!" said Horrocks as he threw the door open, and let fly with the twelve-bore, Tesser squibbing off all six barrels into the dark, as hard as he could pull the trigger.

The furniture was ruined, and the whole Fort was awake; but that was all. No one had been killed, and the banjo was lying on the disheveled bedclothes as usual.

Then Tesser sat down on the veranda, and used language that would have qualified him for the championship of un- limited devils. Horrocks said things, too, but Tesser said the worst.

When the month came to an end, both Horrocks and

Tesser were glad. They held a final council of war, but came to no conclusion.

"Seems to me your best plan would be to make your devil stretch himself. Go down to Bombay with the time-expired men," said Horrocks. "If he really is a devil, he'll come in the train with you."

" 'Tisn't good enough," said Tesser. "Bombay's no fit place to live in at this time of year. But I'll put in for Depot duty at the Hills." And he did.

Now here the tale rests. The devil stayed below, and Tesser went up and was free. If I had invented this story, I should have put in a satisfactory ending—explained the manifestations as somebody's practical joke. My business being to keep to facts, I can only say what I have said. The devil may have been a hoax. If so, it was one of the best ever arranged. If it was not a hoax—but you must settle that for yourselves.

THE GRAY CHAMPION

by *Nathaniel Hawthorne*

Suddenly, there was seen the figure of an ancient man.

⤳ *T*en

THERE was once a time when New England groaned
under the actual pressure of heavier wrongs than those
threatened ones which brought on the revolution. James II,
the bigoted successor of Charles the Voluptuous, had an-
nulled the charters of all the colonies, and sent a harsh and
unprincipled soldier to take away our liberties and endanger
our religion. The administration of Sir Edmund Andros
lacked scarcely a single characteristic of tyranny: a Governor
and Council, holding office from the King, and wholly inde-
pendent of the country; laws made and taxes levied without
concurrence of the people immediate or by their representa-
tives; the rights of private citizens violated, and the titles of
all landed property declared void; the voice of complaint
stifled by restrictions on the press; and, finally, disaffection
overawed by the first band of mercenary troops that ever
marched on our free soil. For two years our ancestors were

kept in sullen submission by that filial love which had in-
variably secured their allegiance to the mother country,
whether its head chanced to be a Parliament, Protector, or
Popish Monarch. Till these evil times, however, such allegiance had been merely nominal, and the colonists had
ruled themselves, enjoying far more freedom than is even
yet the privilege of the native subjects of Great Britain.

At length a rumor reached our shores that the Prince of
Orange had ventured on an enterprise, the success of which
would be the triumph of civil and religious rights and the
salvation of New England. It was but a doubtful whisper; it
might be false, or the attempt might fail; and, in either case,
the man that stirred against King James would lose his head.
Still the intelligence produced a marked effect. The people
smiled mysteriously in the streets, and threw bold glances
at their oppressors; while, far and wide, there was a subdued
and silent agitation, as if the slightest signal would rouse the
whole land from its sluggish despondency. Aware of their
danger, the rulers resolved to avert it by an imposing display
of strength, and perhaps to confirm their despotism by yet
harsher measures. One afternoon in April, 1689, Sir Edmund Andros and his favorite councilors, being warm with
wine, assembled the redcoats of the Governor's Guard, and
made their appearance in the streets of Boston. The sun was
near setting when the march commenced.

The roll of the drum, at that unquiet crisis, seemed to go
through the streets, less as the martial music of the soldiers
than as a muster-call to the inhabitants themselves. A mul-

titude, by various avenues, assembled in King Street, which was destined to be the scene, nearly a century afterwards, of another encounter between the troops of Britain and a people struggling against her tyranny. Though more than sixty years had elapsed since the Pilgrims came, this crowd of their descendants still showed the strong and somber features of their character, perhaps more strikingly in such a stern emergency than on happier occasions. There were the sober garb, the general severity of mien, the gloomy but undismayed expression, the Scriptural forms of speech, and the confidence in Heaven's blessing on a righteous cause, which would have marked a band of the original Puritans, when threatened by some peril of the wilderness. Indeed, it was not yet time for the old spirit to be extinct; since there were men in the street, that day, who had worshipped there beneath the trees, before a house was reared to the God for whom they had become exiles. Old soldiers of the Parliament were here, too, smiling grimly at the thought that their aged arms might strike another blow against the house of Stuart. Here, also, were the veterans of King Philip's war, who had burned villages and slaughtered young and old, with pious fierceness, while the godly souls throughout the land were helping them with prayer. Several ministers were scattered among the crowd, which, unlike all other mobs, regarded them with such reverence, as if there were sanctity in their very garments. These holy men exerted their influence to quiet the people, but not to disperse them. Meantime, the purpose of the Governor, in disturbing the peace of the town, at a period when the slightest commotion might throw the country into a ferment, was almost the universal subject of inquiry, and variously explained.

"Satan will strike his master-stroke presently," cried some, "because he knoweth that his time is short. All our godly pastors are to be dragged to prison! We shall see them at a Smithfield fire in King Street!"

Hereupon the people of each parish gathered closer round their minister, who looked calmly upwards and assumed a more apostolic dignity, as well befitted a candidate for the highest honor of his profession, the crown of martyrdom. It was actually fancied, at that period, that New England might have a John Rodgers of her own, to take the place of that worthy in the Primer.

"The Pope of Rome has given orders for a new St. Bartholomew!" cried the others. "We are to be massacred, man and male child!"

Neither was this rumor wholly discredited, although the wiser class believed the Governor's object somewhat less atrocious. His predecessor under the old charter, Bradstreet, a venerable companion of the first settlers, was known to be in town. There were grounds for conjecturing that Sir Edmund Andros intended, at once, to strike terror by a parade of military force, and to confound the opposite faction by possessing himself of their chief.

"Stand firm for the old charter, Governor!" shouted the crowd, seizing upon the idea. "The good old Governor Bradstreet!"

While this cry was at the loudest, the people were surprised by the well-known figure of Governor Bradstreet himself, a patriarch of nearly ninety, who appeared on the elevated steps of a door, and, with characteristic mildness, besought them to submit to the constituted authorities.

"My children," concluded this venerable person, "do nothing rashly. Cry not aloud, but pray for the welfare of New England, and expect patiently what the Lord will do in this matter!"

The event was soon to be decided. All this time, the roll of the drum had been approaching through Cornhill, louder and deeper, till with reverberations from house to house, and the regular tramp of martial footsteps, it burst into the street. A double rank of soldiers made their appearance, occupying the whole breadth of the passage, with shouldered matchlocks, and matches burning so as to present a row of fires in the dusk. Their steady march was like the progress of a machine that would roll irresistibly over everything in its way. Next, moving slowly, with a confused clatter of hoofs on the pavement, rode a party of mounted gentlemen, the central figure being Sir Edmund Andros, elderly but erect and soldier-like. Those around him were his favorite councilors, and the bitterest foes of New England. At his right hand rode Edward Randolph, our archenemy, that "blasted wretch," as Cotton Mather calls him, who achieved the downfall of our ancient government and was followed with a sensible curse, through life and to his grave. On the other side was Bullivant, scattering jests and mockery as he rode along. Dudley came behind, with a downcast look, dreading, as well he might, to meet the indignant gaze of the people, who beheld him, their only countryman by birth, among the oppressors of his native land. The captain of a frigate in the harbor, and two or three civil officers under the Crown, were also there. But the figure which most attracted the public eye, and stirred up the deepest feeling, was the Episcopal clergyman of King's Chapel, riding haughtily among the magistrates in his priestly vestments, the fitting representative of prelacy and persecution, the union of Church and State, and all those abominations which had driven the Puritans to the wilderness. Another guard of soldiers, in double rank, brought up the rear.

The whole scene was a picture of the condition of New England, and its moral, the deformity of any government that does not grow out of the nature of things and the character of the people. On one side the religious multitude, with their sad visages and dark attire, and on the other, the group of despotic rulers, with the High-Churchman in the midst and here and there a crucifix at their bosoms, all magnificently clad, flushed with wine, proud of unjust authority, and scoffing at the universal groan. And the mercenary soliders, waiting but the word to deluge the street with blood, showed the only means by which obedience could be secured.

"O Lord of Hosts," cried a voice among the crowd, "provide a Champion for thy people!"

This ejaculation was loudly uttered, and served as a herald's cry to introduce a remarkable personage. The crowd had rolled back, and were now huddled together neatly at the extremity of the street, while the soldiers had advanced no more than a third of its length. The intervening space was empty—a paved solitude between lofty edifices, which threw almost a twilight shadow over it. Suddenly, there was seen the figure of an ancient man, who seemed to have emerged from among the people, and was walking by himself along the center of the street, to confront the armed band. He wore the old Puritan dress, a dark cloak and a steeple-crowned hat, in the fashion of at least fifty years before, with a heavy sword upon his thigh, but a staff in his hand to assist the tremulous gait of age.

When at some distance from the multitude, the old man turned slowly round, displaying a face of antique majesty, rendered doubly venerable by the hoary beard that descended on his breast. He made a gesture at once of encouragement and warning, then turned again and resumed his way.

"Who is this gray patriarch?" asked the young men of their sires.

"Who is this venerable brother?" asked the old men among themselves.

But none could make reply. The fathers of the people, those of fourscore years and upwards, were disturbed, deeming it strange that they should forget one of such evident authority, whom they must have known in their early days, the associate of Winthrop and all the old councilors, giving laws, and making prayers, and leading them against the savage. The elderly men ought to have remembered him, too, with locks as gray in their youth as their own were now. And the young! How could he have passed so utterly from their memories—that hoary sire, the relic of long-departed times, whose awful benediction had surely been bestowed on their uncovered heads in childhood?

"Whence did he come? What is his purpose? Who can this old man be?" whispered the wondering crowd.

Meanwhile, the venerable stranger, staff in hand, was pursuing his solitary walk along the center of the street. As he drew near the advancing soldiers, and as the roll of their drum came full upon his ear, the old man raised himself to a loftier mien, while the decrepitude of age seemed to fall from his shoulders, leaving him in gray but unbroken dignity. Now, he marched onward with a warrior's step, keeping time to the military music. Thus the aged form advanced on one side, and the whole parade of soldiers and magistrates on the other, till, when scarcely twenty yards remained between, the old man grasped his staff by the middle and held it before him like a leader's truncheon.

"Stand!" cried he.

The eye, the face, the attitude of command; the solemn, yet warlike peal of that voice, fit either to rule a host in the battlefield or be raised to God in prayer, were irresistible. At the old man's word and outstretched arm, the roll of the drum was hushed at once, and the advancing line stood still.

A tremulous enthusiasm seized upon the multitude. That stately form, combining the leader and the saint, so gray, so dimly seen in such an ancient garb, could only belong to some old champion of the righteous cause, whom the oppressor's drum had summoned from his grave. They raised a shout of awe and exultation, and looked for the deliverance of New England.

The Governor, and the gentlemen of his party, perceiving themselves brought to an unexpected stand, rode hastily forward, as if they would have pressed their snorting and affrighted horses right against the hoary apparition. He, however, blenched not a step, but glancing his severe eye round the group which half encompassed him, at last bent it sternly on Sir Edmund Andros. One would have thought that the dark old man was chief ruler there, and that the Governor and Council, with soldiers at their back, representing the whole power and authority of the Crown, had no alternative but obedience.

"What does this old fellow here?" cried Edward Randolph, fiercely. "On, Sir Edmund! Bid the soldiers forward, and give the dotard the same choice that you give all his countrymen—to stand aside or be trampled on!"

"Nay, nay, let us show respect to the good grandsire," said Bullivant, laughing. "See you not he is some old round-headed dignitary who hath lain asleep these thirty years and knows nothing of the change of times? Doubtless he thinks to put us down with a proclamation in Old Noll's name!"

"Are you mad, old man?" demanded Sir Edmund Andros, in loud and harsh tones. "How dare you stay the march of King James's Governor?"

"I have stayed the march of a king himself, ere now," replied the gray figure, with stern composure. "I am here, Sir Governor, because the cry of an oppressed people hath disturbed me in my secret place; and beseeching this favor earnestly of the Lord, it was vouchsafed me to appear once again on earth, in the good old cause of his saints. And what speak ye of James? There is no longer a Popish tyrant on the throne of England, and by tomorrow noon his name shall be a byword in this very street, where ye would make it a word of terror. Back, thou that wast a Governor, back! With this night thy power is ended—tomorrow, the prison! Back, lest I foretell the scaffold!"

The people had been drawing nearer and nearer, and drinking in the words of their champion, who spoke in accents long disused, like one unaccustomed to converse, except with the dead of many years ago. But his voice stirred their souls. They confronted the soldiers not wholly without arms and ready to convert the very stones of the street into deadly weapons. Sir Edmund Andros looked at the old man; then he cast his hard and cruel eye over the multitude, and beheld them burning with that lurid wrath so difficult to kindle or to quench; and again he fixed his gaze on the aged form, which stood obscurely in an open space, where neither friend nor foe had thrust himself. What were his thoughts, he uttered no word which might discover. But whether the oppressor were overawed by the Gray Champion's look, or perceived his peril in the threatening attitude of the people, it is certain that he gave back, and ordered his soldiers to commence a slow and guarded retreat. Before another sunset, the Governor, and all that rode so proudly with him, were prisoners, and long ere it was known that James had abdicated, King William was proclaimed throughout New England.

But where was the Gray Champion? Some reported that when the troops had gone from King Street and the people were thronging tumultuously in their rear, Bradstreet, the aged Governor, was seen to embrace a form more aged than his own. Others soberly affirmed that, while they marveled at the venerable grandeur of his aspect, the old man had faded from their eyes, melting slowly into the hues of twilight, till, where he stood, there was an empty space. But all agreed that the hoary shape was gone. The men of that generation watched for his reappearance, in sunshine and in twilight, but never saw him more, nor knew when his funeral passed, nor where his gravestone was.

And who was the Gray Champion? Perhaps his name might be found in the records of that stern Court of Justice which passed a sentence too mighty for the age but glorious in all after times for its humbling lesson to the monarch and its high example to the subject. I have heard that, whenever the descendants of the Puritans are to show the spirit of their sires, the old man appears again. When eighty years had passed, he walked once more in King Street. Five years later, in the twilight of an April morning, he stood on the green, beside the meeting-house, at Lexington, where now the obelisk of granite, with a slab of slate inlaid, commemorates the first fallen of the Revolution. And when our fathers were toiling at the breastwork on Bunker's Hill, all through that night the old warrior walked his rounds. Long, long may it be, ere he comes again! His hour is one of darkness, and adversity, and peril. But should domestic tyranny oppress us, or the invader's step pollute our soil, still may the Gray Champion come, for he is the type of New England's hereditary spirit, and his shadowy march, on the eve of danger, must ever be the pledge that New England's sons will vindicate their ancestry.

HAMLET'S GHOST

by William Shakespeare

"Be thou a spirit of health or goblin damned . . . ?"

$\succ$ *Eleven*

HAMLET, *son to the late, and nephew to the present king of Denmark.*
HORATIO, *friend to* HAMLET
MARCELLUS ⎫
BERNARDO ⎭ *officers*
FRANCISCO, *a soldier*
GHOST *of* HAMLET's *father*

SCENE: Denmark

ACT I

SCENE I: *Elsinore. A platform before the castle.*

FRANCISCO *at his post. Enter to him* BERNARDO.

BERNARDO: Who's there?

FRANCISCO: Nay, answer me: stand, and unfold yourself.

BERNARDO: Long live the king!

FRANCISCO: Bernardo?

BERNARDO: He.

FRANCISCO: You come most carefully upon your hour.

BERNARDO: 'Tis now struck twelve; get thee to bed, Francisco.

FRANCISCO: For this relief much thanks. 'Tis bitter cold, and I am sick at heart.

BERNARDO: Have you had quiet guard?

FRANCISCO: Not a mouse stirring.

BERNARDO: Well, good night. If you do meet Horatio and Marcellus, the rivals of my watch, bid them make haste.

FRANCISCO: I think I hear them. Stand, ho! Who's there?

Enter HORATIO *and* MARCELLUS

HORATIO: Friends to this ground.

MARCELLUS: And liegemen to the Dane.

FRANCISCO: Give you good night.

MARCELLUS: O, farewell, honest soldier: who hath relieved you?

FRANCISCO: Bernardo has my place. Give you good night.

Exit

MARCELLUS: Holla! Bernardo!

BERNARDO: Say, what, is Horatio there?

HORATIO: A piece of him.

BERNARDO: Welcome, Horatio: welcome, good Marcellus.

MARCELLUS: What, has this thing appeared again tonight?

BERNARDO: I have seen nothing.

MARCELLUS: Horatio says 'tis but our fantasy, and will not let belief take hold of him touching this dreaded sight, twice seen of us: therefore I have entreated him along with us to watch the minutes of this night; that if again this apparition come, he may approve our eyes and speak to it.

HORATIO: Tush, tush, 'twill not appear.

BERNARDO: Sit down a while; and let us once again assail your ears, that are so fortified against our story what we have two nights seen.

HORATIO: Well, sit we down, and let us hear Bernardo speak of this.

BERNARDO: Last night of all, when yond same star that's westward from the pole had made his course to illumine that part of heaven where now it burns, Marcellus and myself, the bell then beating one——

Enter GHOST

MARCELLUS: Peace, break thee off; look, where it comes again!

BERNARDO: In the same figure, like the king that's dead.

MARCELLUS: Thou art a scholar; speak to it, Horatio.

BERNARDO: Looks it not like the king? mark it, Horatio.

HORATIO: Most like: it harrows me with fear and wonder.

BERNARDO: It would be spoke to.

MARCELLUS: Question it, Horatio.

HORATIO: What art thou that usurp'st this time of night, together with that fair and warlike form in which the majesty of buried Denmark did sometimes march? by heaven I charge thee, speak!

MARCELLUS: It is offended.

BERNARDO: See, it stalks away!

HORATIO: Stay! speak, speak! I charge thee, speak!

Exit GHOST

MARCELLUS: 'Tis gone, and will not answer.

BERNARDO: How, now, Horatio! you tremble and look pale: Is not this something more than fantasy? What think you on't?

HORATIO: Before my God, I might not this believe without the sensible and true avouch of mine own eyes.

MARCELLUS: Is it not like the king?

HORATIO: As thou art to thyself. Such was the very armor he had on when he the ambitious Norway combated; so frowned he once, when, in an angry parle, he smote the sledded Polacks on the ice. 'Tis strange.

MARCELLUS: Thus twice before, and jump at this dead hour, with martial stalk hath he gone by our watch.

    •   •   •   •   •

HORATIO: But soft, behold! lo, where it comes again!

Re-enter GHOST

I'll cross it, though it blast me. Stay, illusion! If thou hast any sound, or use of voice, speak to me: if there be any good thing to be done, that may to thee do ease and grace to me, speak to me.

Cock crows

Speak of it: stay, and speak! Stop it, Marcellus.
MARCELLUS: Shall I strike at it with my partisan?
HORATIO: Do, if it will not stand.
BERNARDO: 'Tis here!
HORATIO: 'Tis here!

Exit GHOST

MARCELLUS: 'Tis gone! We do it wrong, being so majestical, to offer it the show of violence; for it is, as the air, invulnerable, and our vain blows malicious mockery.
BERNARDO: It was about to speak, when the cock crew.
HORATIO: And then it started like a guilty thing upon a fearful summons. I have heard the cock, that is the trumpet to the morn, doth with his lofty and shrill-sounding throat awake the god of day; and, at his warning, whether in sea or fire, in earth or air, the extravagant and erring spirit hies to his confine; and of the truth herein this present object made probation.
MARCELLUS: It faded on the crowing of the cock. Some say that ever 'gainst that season comes wherein our Saviour's birth is celebrated, the bird of dawning singeth all night

long. And then, they say, no spirit dares stir abroad; the nights are wholesome; then no planets strike, no fairy takes, nor witch hath power to charm, so hallowed and so gracious is the time.

HORATIO: So I have heard and do in part believe it. But, look, the morn in russet mantle clad, walks o'er the dew of yon high eastern hill. Break we our watch up; and by my advice, let us impart what we have seen tonight unto young Hamlet; for, upon my life, this spirit, dumb to us, will speak to him. Do you consent we shall acquaint him with it, as needful in our loves, fitting our duty?

MARCELLUS: Let's do't, I pray; and I this morning know where we shall find him most conveniently.

Exeunt

SCENE II: *A room of state in the castle.* *HAMLET *is alone in the room.*

Enter HORATIO, MARCELLUS, *and* BERNARDO

HORATIO: Hail to your lordship!

HAMLET: I am glad to see you well. Horatio—or do I forget myself?

HORATIO: The same, my lord, and your poor servant ever.

HAMLET: Sir, my good friend; I'll change that name with you. And what makes you from Wittenberg, Horatio? Marcellus?

MARCELLUS: My good lord——

* Editor's note.

HAMLET: I am very glad to see you. Good even, sir. But what, in faith, make you from Wittenberg?

HORATIO: A truant disposition, good my lord.

HAMLET: I would not hear your enemy say so, nor shall you do mine ear that violence, to make it truster of your own report against yourself; I know you are no truant. But what is your affair in Elsinore? We'll teach you to drink deep ere you depart.

HORATIO: My lord, I came to see your father's funeral.

HAMLET: I pray thee, do not mock me, fellow-student; I think it was to see my mother's wedding.

HORATIO: Indeed, my lord, it followed hard upon.

HAMLET: Thrift, thrift, Horatio! the funeral baked meats did coldly furnish forth the marriage tables. Would I had met my dearest foe in heaven or ever I had seen that day, Horatio! My father!—methinks I see my father.

HORATIO: Where, my lord?

HAMLET: In my mind's eye, Horatio.

HORATIO: I saw him once; he was a goodly king.

HAMLET: He was a man, take him for all in all, I shall not look upon his like again.

HORATIO: My lord, I think I saw him yesternight.

HAMLET: Saw? who?

HORATIO: My lord, the king, your father.

HAMLET: The king my father!

HORATIO: Season your admiration for a while with an attent ear, till I may deliver, upon the witness of these gentlemen, this marvel to you.

HAMLET: For God's love, let me hear.

HORATIO: Two nights together had these gentlemen, Marcellus and Bernardo, on their watch, in the dead vast and middle of the night, been thus encountered. A figure like your father, armed at point exactly, cap-a-pe, appears before them, and with solemn march goes slow and stately by them. Thrice he walked by their oppressed and fear-surprised eyes, within his truncheon's length; whilst they, distilled almost to jelly with the act of fear, stand dumb and speak not to him. This to me in dreadful secrecy impart they did; and I with them the third night kept the watch; where, as they had delivered, both in time, form of the thing, each word made true and good, the apparition comes. I knew your father; these hands are not more like.

HAMLET: But where was this?

MARCELLUS: My lord, upon the platform where we watched.

HAMLET: Did you not speak to it?

HORATIO: My lord, I did; but answer made it none: yet once methought it lifted up its head and did address itself to motion, like as it would speak; but even then the morning cock crew loud, and at the sound it shrunk in haste away, and vanished from our sight.

HAMLET: 'Tis very strange.

HORATIO: As I do live, my honored lord, 'tis true; and we did think it writ down in our duty to let you know of it.

HAMLET: Indeed, indeed, sirs, but this troubles me. Hold you the watch tonight?

MARCELLUS:
BERNARDO: } We do, my lord.

HAMLET: Armed, say you?

MARCELLUS:
BERNARDO: } Armed, my lord.

HAMLET: From top to toe?

MARCELLUS:
BERNARDO: } My lord, from head to foot.

HAMLET: Then saw you not his face?

HORATIO: O, yes, my lord; he wore his beaver up.

HAMLET: What, looked he frowningly?

HORATIO: A countenance more in sorrow than in anger.

HAMLET: Pale or red?

HORATIO: Nay, very pale.

HAMLET: And fixed his eyes upon you?

HORATIO: Most constantly.

HAMLET: I would I had been there.

HORATIO: It would have much amazed you.

HAMLET: Very like, very like. Stayed it long?

HORATIO: While one with moderate haste might tell a hundred.

MARCELLUS:
BERNARDO: } Longer, longer.

HORATIO: Not when I saw it.

HAMLET: His beard was grizzled—no?

HORATIO: It was, as I have seen it in his life, a sable silvered.

HAMLET: I will watch tonight; perchance 'twill walk again.

HORATIO: I warrant it will.

HAMLET: If it assume my noble father's person, I'll speak to it though hell itself should gape and bid me hold my peace. I pray you all, if you have hitherto concealed this sight, let it be tenable in your silence still; and whatsoever else shall hap tonight, give it an understanding, but no tongue. I will requite your loves. So, fare you well. Upon the platform, 'twixt eleven and twelve, I'll visit you.

ALL: Our duty to your honor.

HAMLET: Your loves, as mine to you: farewell.

Exeunt all but HAMLET

My father's spirit in arms! all is not well; I doubt some foul play. Would the night were come! Till then sit still, my soul; foul deeds will rise, though all the earth o'erwhelm them, to men's eyes.

Exit

Scene IV: *The platform*

Enter HAMLET, HORATIO, *and* MARCELLUS

HAMLET: The air bites shrewdly; it is very cold.

HORATIO: It is a nipping and an eager air.

HAMLET: What hour now?

HORATIO: I think it lacks of twelve.

HAMLET: No, it is struck.

HORATIO: Indeed? I heard it not. Then it draws near the season wherein the spirit held his wont to walk.
Look, my lord, it comes!

Enter GHOST

HAMLET: Angels and ministers of grace defend us! Be thou a spirit of health or goblin damned, bring with thee airs from heaven or blasts from hell, be thy intents wicked or charitable, thou comest in such a questionable shape that I will speak to thee. I'll call thee Hamlet, King, father, royal Dane. O, answer me! Let me not burst in ignorance; but tell why thy canonized bones, hearsed in death, have burst their cerements; why the sepulchre, wherein we saw thee quietly inurned, hath oped his ponderous and noble jaws, to cast thee up again. What may this mean, that thou, dead corpse, again in complete steel revisitest thus the glimpses of the moon, making night hideous; and we fools of nature so horridly to shake our disposition with thoughts beyond the reaches of our souls? Say, why is this? wherefore? what should we do?

GHOST *beckons* HAMLET

HORATIO: It beckons you to go away with it, as if it some impartment did desire to you alone.

MARCELLUS: Look, with what courteous action it waves you
to a more removed ground. But do not go with it.

HORATIO: No, by no means.

HAMLET: It will not speak, then I will follow it.

HORATIO: Do not, my lord.

HAMLET: Why, what should be the fear? I do not set my
life at a pin's fee; and for my soul, what can it do to that,
being a thing immortal as itself? It waves me forth again;
I'll follow it.

HORATIO: What if it tempt you toward the flood, my lord,
or to the dreadful summit of the cliff that beetles o'er his
base into the sea, and there assume some other horrible
form, which might deprive your sovereignty of reason and
draw you into madness? think of it. The very place puts
toys of desperation, without more motive, into every
brain that looks so many fathoms to the sea and hears it
roar beneath.

HAMLET: It waves me still. Go on; I'll follow thee.

MARCELLUS: You shall not go, my lord.

HAMLET: Hold off your hands.

HORATIO: Be ruled; you shall not go.

HAMLET: My fate cries out, and makes each petty artery in
this body as hardy as the Nemean lion's nerve. Still am I
called. Unhand me, gentlemen. By heaven, I'll make a
ghost of him that lets me! I say, away! Go on: I'll follow
thee.

Exeunt GHOST *and* HAMLET

HORATIO: He waxes desperate with imagination.

MARCELLUS: Let's follow; 'tis not fit thus to obey him.

HORATIO: Have after. To what issue will this come?

MARCELLUS: Something is rotten in the state of Denmark.

HORATIO: Heaven will direct it.

MARCELLUS: Nay, let's follow him.

Exeunt

Scene V: *Another part of the platform*

Enter GHOST *and* HAMLET

HAMLET: Where wilt thou lead me? speak; I'll go no further.

GHOST: Mark me.

HAMLET: I will.

GHOST: My hour is almost come when I to sulphurous and tormenting flames must render up myself.

HAMLET: Alas, poor ghost!

GHOST: Pity me not, but lend thy serious hearing to what I shall unfold.

HAMLET: Speak; I am bound to hear.

GHOST: So art thou to revenge, when thou shalt hear.

HAMLET: What?

GHOST: I am thy father's spirit, doomed for a certain term to walk the night, and for the day confined to fast in fires, till the foul crimes done in my days of nature are burnt and purged away. But that I am forbid to tell the secrets

of my prison-house, I could a tale unfold whose lightest
word would harrow up thy soul, freeze thy young blood,
make thy two eyes, like stars, start from their spheres, thy
knotted and combined locks to part and each particular
hair to stand on end, like quills upon the fretful porpen-
tine. But this eternal blazon must not be to ears of flesh
and blood. List, list, O, list! If thou didst ever thy dear
father love——

HAMLET: O God!

GHOST: Revenge his foul and most unnatural murder.

HAMLET: Murder!

GHOST: Murder most foul, as in the best it is; but this most
foul, strange and unnatural.

HAMLET: Haste me to know it, that I, with wings as swift
as meditation or the thoughts of love, may sweep to my
revenge.

GHOST: I find thee apt; and duller shouldst thou be than
the fat weed that roots itself in ease on Lethe wharf,
wouldst thou not stir in this. Now, Hamlet, hear: 'Tis
given out that, sleeping in my orchard, a serpent stung
me; so the whole ear of Denmark is by a forged process
of my death rankly abused: but know, thou noble youth,
the serpent that did sting thy father's life now wears his
crown.

HAMLET: O my prophetic soul!

GHOST: But, soft! methinks I scent the morning air; brief
let me be. Sleeping within my orchard, my custom always
in the afternoon, upon my secure hour thy uncle stole,

with juice of cursed hebenon in a vial, and in the porches of my ears did pour the leperous distilment; whose effect holds such an enmity with blood of man that swift as quicksilver it courses through the natural gates and alleys of the body, and with a sudden vigor it doth posset and curd, like eager droppings into milk, the thin and wholesome blood. So did it mine. Thus was I, sleeping, by a brother's hand of life, of crown, of queen, at once dispatched; cut off even in the blossoms of my sin, no reckoning made, but sent to my account with all my imperfections on my head. O, horrible! O, horrible! most horrible! If thou hast nature in thee bear it not; but, howsoever thou pursuest this act, taint not thy mind, nor let thy soul contrive against thy mother aught. Leave her to heaven and to those thorns that in her bosom lodge, to prick and sting her.

Fare thee well at once! The glow-worm shows the matin to be near, and 'gins to pale his uneffectual fire. Adieu, adieu! Hamlet, remember me.

Exit

HAMLET: O all you host of heaven! O earth! what else? And shall I couple hell? O, fie! Hold, hold, my heart; and you, my sinews, grow not instant old, but bear me stiffly up. Remember thee! Ay, thou poor ghost, while memory holds a seat in this distracted globe. Remember thee! Yea, from the table of my memory I'll wipe away all trivial fond records, all saws of books, all forms, all pressures past, that youth and observation copied there; and thy commandment all alone shall live within the book and volume of my brain, unmixed with baser matter: yes, by heaven!

O most pernicious woman!

O villain, villain, smiling, damned villain!

My tables—meet it as I set it down, that one may smile, and smile, and be a villain; at least I'm sure it may be so in Denmark. So, uncle, there you are. Now to my word; it is 'Adieu, adieu! remember me.' I have sworn it.

MARCELLUS:}
HORATIO:} *(within)* My lord, my lord——

MARCELLUS: *(within)* Lord Hamlet——

HORATIO: *(within)* Heaven secure him!

HAMLET: So be it!

HORATIO: *(within)* Hillo, ho, ho, my lord!

HAMLET: Hillo, ho, ho, boy! come, bird, come.

Enter HORATIO *and* MARCELLUS

MARCELLUS: How is it, my noble lord?

HORATIO: What news, my lord?

HAMLET: O, wonderful!

HORATIO: Good, my lord, tell it.

HAMLET: No; you'll reveal it.

HORATIO: Not I, my lord, by heaven.

MARCELLUS: Not I, my lord.

HAMLET: How say you, then; would heart of man once think it? But you'll be secret?

HORATIO:
MARCELLUS: } Ay, by heaven, my lord.

HAMLET: There's ne'er a villain dwelling in all Denmark but he's an arrant knave.

HORATIO: There needs no ghost, my lord, come from the grave to tell us this.

HAMLET: Why, right; you are in the right; and so, without more circumstance at all, I hold it fit that we shake hands and part: you, as your business and desire shall point you; for every man has business and desire, such as it is; and for mine own part, look you, I'll go pray.

HORATIO: These are but wild and whirling words, my lord.

HAMLET: I'm sorry they offend you, heartily; yes, 'faith, heartily.

HORATIO: There's no offense, my lord.

HAMLET: Yes, by Saint Patrick, but there is, Horatio, and much offense too. Touching this vision here, it is an honest ghost, that let me tell you: for your desire to know what is between us, o'ermaster it as you many. And now, good friends, as you are friends, scholars and soldiers, give me one poor request.

HORATIO: What is it, my lord? we will.

HAMLET: Never make known what you have seen tonight.

HORATIO:
MARCELLUS: } My lord, we will not.

HAMLET: Nay, but swear it.

HORATIO: In faith, my lord, not I.

MARCELLUS: Nor I, my lord, in faith.

HAMLET: Upon my sword.

MARCELLUS: We have sworn, my lord, already.

HAMLET: Indeed, upon my sword, indeed.

GHOST: (*beneath*) Swear.

HAMLET: Ah, ha, boy! say'st thou so? art thou there, true-penny? Come on—you hear this fellow in the cellarage—consent to swear.

HORATIO: Propose the oath, my lord.

HAMLET: Never to speak of this that you have seen, swear by my sword.

GHOST:(*beneath*) Swear.

HAMLET: *Hic et ubique?* Then we'll shift our ground. Come hither, gentlemen, and lay your hands again upon my sword: never to speak of this that you have heard, swear by my sword.

GHOST: (*beneath*) Swear.

HAMLET: Well said, old mole! canst work in the earth so fast? A worthy pioneer! Once more remove, good friends.

HORATIO: O day and night, but this is wondrous strange!

HAMLET: And therefore as a stranger give it welcome. There are more things in heaven and earth, Horatio, than are dreamt of in your philosophy. But come; here, as before, never, so help you mercy, how strange or odd soe'er I bear myself, as I perchance hereafter shall think meet to put an antic disposition on, that you, at such times seeing me, never shall, with arms encumbered thus, or this headshake, or by pronouncing of some doubtful phrase, as 'Well, well, we know,' or, 'We could, an if we would,' or 'If we list to speak,' or 'There be, an if they might,' or such ambiguous giving out, to note that you know aught of me: this not to do, so grace and mercy at your most need help you, swear.

GHOST: (*beneath*) Swear.

HAMLET: Rest, rest, perturbed spirit! (*They swear.*) So, gentlemen, with all my love I do commend me to you; and what so poor a man as Hamlet is may do, to express his love and friending to you, God willing, shall not lack. Let us go in together; and still your fingers on your lips, I pray. The time is out of joint: O cursed spite, that ever I was born to set it right! Nay, come, let's go together.

Exeunt

MARLEY'S GHOST

by Charles Dickens

It came on through the heavy door and passed into the room before his eyes.

$\succ$ *T*$_{welve}$

MARLEY was dead, to begin with. There is no doubt whatever about that. The register of his burial was signed by the clergyman, the clerk, the undertaker, and the chief mourner. Scrooge signed it. And Scrooge's name was good upon 'Change for anything he chose to put his hand to. Old Marley was as dead as a door-nail.

Mind! I don't mean to say that I know of my own knowledge, what there is particularly dead about a door-nail. I might have been inclined, myself, to regard a coffin-nail as the deadest piece of ironmongery in the trade. But the wisdom of our ancestors is in the simile; and my unhallowed hands shall not disturb it, or the country's done for. You will, therefore, permit me to repeat, emphatically, that Marley was as dead as a door-nail.

Scrooge knew he was dead? Of course he did. How could it be otherwise? Scrooge and he were partners for I don't know how many years. Scrooge was his sole executor, his sole administrator, his sole assign, his sole residuary legatee, his sole friend, and sole mourner. And even Scrooge was not so dreadfully cut up by the sad event but that he was an excellent man of business on the very day of the funeral, and solemnized it with an undoubted bargain.

The mention of Marley's funeral brings me back to the point I started from. There is no doubt that Marley was dead. This must be distinctly understood, or nothing wonderful can come of the story I am going to relate. If we were not perfectly convinced that Hamlet's father died before the play began, there would be nothing more remarkable in his taking a stroll at night, in an easterly wind, upon his own ramparts, than there would be in any other middle-aged gentleman rashly turning out after dark in a breezy spot— say St. Paul's Churchyard, for instance—literally to astonish his son's weak mind.

Scrooge never painted out Old Marley's name. There it stood, years afterward, above the warehouse door: Scrooge and Marley. The firm was known as Scrooge and Marley. Sometimes people new to the business called Scrooge Scrooge, and sometimes Marley, but he answered to both names. It was all the same to him.

Oh! but he was a tight-fisted hand at the grindstone, Scrooge! a squeezing, wrenching, grasping, scraping, clutching, covetous old sinner! Hard and sharp as flint, from which no steel had ever struck out generous fire; secret, and self-contained, and solitary as an oyster. The cold within him froze his old features, nipped his pointed nose, shriveled his cheek, stiffened his gait; made his eyes red, his thin lips blue; and spoke out shrewdly in his grating voice. A frosty rime was on his head, and on his eyebrows, and his wiry chin. He carried his own low temperature always about with him; he iced his office in the dog-days, and didn't thaw it one degree at Christmas.

External heat and cold had little influence on Scrooge. No warmth could warm, no wintry weather chill him. No wind that blew was bitterer than he, no falling snow was more intent upon its purpose, no pelting rain less open to entreaty. Foul weather didn't know where to have him. The heaviest rain, and snow, and hail, and sleet could boast of the advantage over him in only one respect. They often "came down" handsomely, and Scrooge never did.

Nobody ever stopped him in the street to say, with gladsome looks, "My dear Scrooge, how are you? When will you come to see me?" No beggars implored him to bestow a trifle, no children asked him what it was o'clock, no man or woman ever once in all his life inquired the way to such and such a place, of Scrooge. Even the blind men's dogs appeared to know him; and, when they saw him coming on, would tug their owners into doorways and up courts; and then would wag their tails as though they said, "No eye at all is better than an evil eye, dark master!"

But what did Scrooge care? It was the very thing he liked.

To edge his way along the crowded paths of life, warning all human sympathy to keep its distance, was what the knowing ones call "nuts" to Scrooge.

Once upon a time—of all the good days in the year, on Christmas Eve—old Scrooge sat busy in his counting-house. It was cold, bleak, biting weather; foggy withal; and he could hear the people in the court outside go wheezing up and down, beating their hands upon their breasts, and stamping their feet upon the pavement stones to warm them. The City clocks had only just gone three, but it was quite dark already—it had not been light all day—and candles were flaring in the windows of the neighboring offices, like ruddy smears upon the palpable brown air. The fog came pouring in at every chink and keyhole, and was so dense without, that, although the court was of the narrowest, the houses opposite were mere phantoms. To see the dingy cloud come drooping down, obscuring everything, one might have thought that nature lived hard by, and was brewing on a large scale.

The door of Scrooge's counting-house was open, that he might keep his eye upon his clerk, who in a dismal little cell beyond, a sort of tank, was copying letters. Scrooge had a very small fire, but the clerk's fire was so very much smaller that it looked like one coal. But he couldn't replenish it, for Scrooge kept the coal-box in his own room; and so surely as the clerk came in with the shovel, the master predicted that it would be necessary for them to part. Wherefore the clerk put on his white comforter, and tried to warm himself at the candle; in which effort, not being a man of strong imagination, he failed.

At length the hour of shutting up the counting-house arrived. With an ill-will Scrooge dismounted from his stool, and tacitly admitted the fact to the expectant clerk in the tank, who instantly snuffed his candle out, and put on his hat.

"You'll want all day tomorrow, I suppose?" said Scrooge.

"If quite convenient, sir."

"It's not convenient," said Scrooge, "and it's not fair. If I was to stop half-a-crown for it, you'd think yourself ill used, I'll be bound?"

The clerk smiled faintly.

"And yet," said Scrooge, "you don't think *me* ill used when I pay a day's wages for no work."

The clerk observed that it was only once a year.

"A poor excuse for picking a man's pocket every twenty-fifth of December!" said Scrooge, buttoning his greatcoat to the chin. "But I suppose you must have the whole day. Be here all the earlier next morning."

The clerk promised that he would; and Scrooge walked out with a growl.

Scrooge took his melancholy dinner in his usual melancholy tavern; and having read all the newspapers, and beguiled the rest of the evening with his banker's book, went home to bed. He lived in chambers which had once belonged to his deceased partner. They were a gloomy suite of rooms, in a lowering pile of building up a yard, where it had so little business to be, that one could scarcely help fancying it must have run there when it was a young house, playing at hide-and-seek with other houses, and have forgotten the way out again. It was old enough now, and dreary enough; for nobody lived in it but Scrooge, the other rooms being all let out as offices. The yard was so dark that even Scrooge, who knew its every stone, was fain to grope with his hands. The fog and frost so hung about the black old gateway of the house that it seemed as if the Genius of the Weather sat in mournful meditation on the threshold.

Now, it is a fact that there was nothing at all particular about the knocker on the door, except that it was very large. It is also a fact that Scrooge had seen it, night and morning, during his whole residence in that place; also that Scrooge had as little of what is called fancy about him as any man in the City of London, even including—which is a bold word—the corporation, aldermen, and livery. Let it also be borne in mind that Scrooge had not bestowed one thought on Marley since his last mention of his seven-years-dead partner that afternoon. And then let any man explain to me, if he can, how it happened that Scrooge, having the key in the lock of the door, saw in the knocker, without its undergoing any intermediate process of change—not a knocker, but Marley's face.

Marley's face. It was not in impenetrable shadow, as the other objects in the yard were, but had a dismal light about it, like a bad lobster in a dark cellar. It was not angry or ferocious, but looked at Scrooge as Marley used to look; with ghostly spectacles turned up on its ghostly forehead. The hair was curiously stirred, as if by breath or hot air; and, though the eyes were wide open, they were perfectly motionless. That, and its livid color, made it horrible; but its horror seemed to be in spite of the face, and beyond its control, rather than a part of its own expression.

As Scrooge looked fixedly at this phenomenon, it was a knocker again.

To say that he was not startled, or that his blood was not conscious of a terrible sensation to which it had been a stranger from infancy, would be untrue. But he put his hand upon the key he had relinquished, turned it sturdily, walked in, and lighted his candle.

He *did* pause, with a moment's irresolution, before he shut the door; and he *did* look cautiously behind it first, as if he half expected to be terrified with the sight of Marley's pigtail sticking out into the hall. But there was nothing on the back of the door except the screws and nuts that held the knocker on, so he said, "Pooh, pooh!" and closed it with a bang.

The sound resounded through the house like thunder. Every room above, and every cask in the wine-merchant's cellars below, appeared to have a separate peal of echoes of its own. Scrooge was not a man to be frightened by echoes. He fastened the door, and walked across the hall and up the stairs: slowly, too: trimming his candle as he went.

You may talk vaguely about driving a coach and six up a

good old flight of stairs or through a bad young Act of Parliament; but I mean to say you might have got a hearse up that staircase, and taken it broadwise, with the splinter-bar towards the wall and the door towards the balustrades, and done it easy. There was plenty of width for that, and room to spare; which is perhaps the reason why Scrooge thought he saw a locomotive hearse going on before him in the gloom. Half-a-dozen gas-lamps out of the street wouldn't have lighted the entry too well, so you may suppose that it was pretty dark with Scrooge's dip.

Up Scrooge went, not caring a button for that. Darkness is cheap, and Scrooge liked it. But before he shut his heavy door he walked through his rooms to see that all was right. He had just enough recollection of the face to desire to do that.

Sitting-room, bedroom, lumber-room. All as they should be. Nobody under the table, nobody under the sofa; a small fire in the grate; spoon and basin ready; and the little sauce-pan of gruel (Scrooge had a cold in his head) upon the hob. Nobody under the bed; nobody in the closet; nobody in his dressing-gown, which was hanging up in a suspicious attitude against the wall. Lumber-room as usual. Old fire-guard, old shoes, two fish baskets, washing-stand on three legs, and a poker.

Quite satisfied, he closed his door, and locked himself in; double locked himself in, which was not his custom. Thus secured against surprise, he took off his cravat; put on his dressing-gown and slippers, and his nightcap; and sat down before the fire to take his gruel.

It was a very low fire indeed; nothing on such a bitter night. He was obliged to sit close to it, and brood over it, before he could extract the least sensation of warmth from such a handful of fuel. The fireplace was an old one, built by some Dutch merchant long ago and paved all round with quaint Dutch tiles designed to illustrate the Scriptures. There were Cains and Abels, Pharaoh's daughters, Queens of Sheba, Angelic messengers descending through the air on clouds like featherbeds, Abrahams, Belshazzars, Apostles putting off to sea in butter-boats, hundreds of figures to attract his thoughts; and yet that face of Marley, seven years dead, came like the ancient Prophet's rod, and swallowed up the whole. If each smooth tile had been a blank at first, with power to shape some picture on its surface from the disjointed fragments, there would have been a copy of old Marley's head on every one.

"Humbug!" said Scrooge; and walked across the room.

After several turns he sat down again. As he threw his head back in the chair, his glance happened to rest upon a bell, a disused bell, that hung in the room, and communicated, for some purpose now forgotten, with a chamber in the highest storey of the building. It was with great astonishment, and with a strange, inexplicable dread, that, as he looked, he saw this bell begin to swing. It swung so softly in the outset that it scarcely made a sound, but soon it rang out loudly, and so did every bell in the house.

This might have lasted half a minute, or a minute, but it seemed an hour. The bells ceased, as they had begun, together. They were succeeded by a clanking noise deep down below as if some person were dragging a heavy chain over the casks in the wine-merchant's cellar. Scrooge then remembered to have heard that ghosts in haunted houses were described as dragging chains.

The cellar door flew open with a booming sound, and then he heard the noise much louder on the floors below; then coming up the stairs; then coming straight towards his door.

"It's humbug still!" said Scrooge. "I won't believe it."

His color changed, though, when, without a pause, it came on through the heavy door and passed into the room before his eyes. Upon its coming in, the dying flame leaped up, as though it cried, "I know him! Marley's Ghost!" and fell again.

The same face: the very same. Marley in his pigtail, usual waistcoat, tights, and boots; the tassels on the latter bristling, like his pigtail, and his coat-skirts, and the hair upon his head. The chain he drew was clasped about his middle. It was long, and wound about him like a tail; and it was made (for Scrooge observed it closely) of cash-boxes, keys, padlocks, ledgers, deeds, and heavy purses wrought in steel. His body was transparent; so that Scrooge, observing him, and looking through his waistcoat, could see the two buttons on his coat behind.

Scrooge had often heard it said that Marley had no bowels, but he had never believed it until now.

No, nor did he believe it even now. Though he looked the phantom through and through, and saw it standing before him; though he felt the chilling influence of its death-cold eyes, and marked the very texture of the folded kerchief bound about its head and chin, which wrapper he had not observed before, he was still incredulous, and fought against his senses.

"How now!" said Scrooge, caustic and cold as ever. "What do you want with me?"

"Much!"—Marley's voice; no doubt about it.

"Who are you?"

"Ask me who I *was*."

"Who *were* you, then?" said Scrooge, raising his voice. "You're particular, for a shade." He was going to say "*to* a shade," but substituted this, as more appropriate.

"In life I was your partner, Jacob Marley."

"Can you—can you sit down?" asked Scrooge, looking doubtfully at him.

"I can."

"Do it, then."

Scrooge asked the question, because he didn't know whether a ghost so transparent might find himself in a condition to take a chair; and felt that in the event of its being impossible, it might involve the necessity of an embarrassing explanation. But the Ghost sat down on the opposite side of the fireplace, as if he were quite used to it.

"You don't believe in me," observed the Ghost.

"I don't," said Scrooge.

"What evidence would you have of my reality beyond that of your own senses?"

"I don't know," said Scrooge.

"Why do you doubt your senses?"

"Because," said Scrooge, "a little thing affects them. A slight disorder of the stomach makes them cheats. You may be an undigested bit of beef, a blot of mustard, a crumb of cheese, a fragment of an underdone potato. There's more of gravy than of grave about you, whatever you are!"

Scrooge was not much in the habit of cracking jokes, nor did he feel in his heart by any means waggish then. The truth is that he tried to be smart as a means of distracting his own attention and keeping down his terror; for the spectre's voice disturbed the very marrow in his bones.

To sit staring at those fixed, glazed eyes in silence, for a moment, would play, Scrooge felt, the very deuce with him. There was something very awful, too, in the spectre's being provided with an infernal atmosphere of his own. Scrooge could not feel it himself, but this was clearly the case; for though the Ghost sat perfectly motionless, its hair, and skirts, and tassels were still agitated as by the hot vapor from an oven.

"You see this toothpick?" said Scrooge, returning quickly to the charge, for the reason just assigned; and wishing, though it were only for a second, to divert the vision's stony gaze from himself.

"I do," replied the Ghost.

"You are not looking at it," said Scrooge.

"But I see it," said the Ghost, "notwithstanding."

"Well!" returned Scrooge, "I have but to swallow this,

and be for the rest of my days persecuted by a legion of goblins, all of my own creation. Humbug, I tell you: humbug!"

At this the spirit raised a frightful cry, and shook its chain with such a dismal and appalling noise that Scrooge held on tight to his chair to save himself from falling in a swoon. But how much greater was his horror when the phantom, taking off the bandage round its head, as if it were too warm to wear indoors, its lower jaw dropped down upon its breast!

Scrooge fell upon his knees and clasped his hands before his face.

"Mercy!" he said. "Dreadful apparition, why do you trouble me?"

"Man of the worldly mind!" replied the Ghost, "do you believe in me or not?"

"I do," said Scrooge; "I must. But why do spirits walk the earth, and why do they come to me?"

"It is required of every man," the Ghost returned, "that the spirit within him should walk abroad among his fellow-men, and travel far and wide; and, if that spirit goes not forth in life, it is condemned to do so after death. It is doomed to wander through the world—oh, woe is me!—and witness what it cannot share, but might have shared on earth, and turned to happiness!"

Again the spectre raised a cry, and shook its chain and wrung its shadowy hands.

"You are fettered," said Scrooge, trembling. "Tell me why?"

"I wear the chain I forged in life," replied the Ghost. "I made it link by link, and yard by yard; I girded it on of my own free will, and of my own free will I wore it. Is its pattern strange to *you?*"

Scrooge trembled more and more.

"Or would you know," pursued the Ghost, "the weight and length of the strong coil you bear yourself? It was full as heavy and as long as this seven Christmas Eves ago. You have labored on it since. It is a ponderous chain!"

Scrooge glanced about him on the floor, in the expectation of finding himself surrounded by some fifty or sixty fathoms of iron cable; but he could see nothing.

"Jacob!" he said imploringly. "Old Jacob Marley, tell me more! Speak comfort to me, Jacob!"

"I have none to give," the Ghost replied. "It comes from other regions, Ebenezer Scrooge, and is conveyed by other ministers to other kinds of men. Nor can I tell you what I would. A very little more is all permitted to me. I cannot rest, I cannot stay, I cannot linger anywhere. My spirit never walked beyond our counting-house—mark me—in life my spirit never roved beyond the narrow limits of our money-changing hole; and weary journeys lie before me!"

It was a habit with Scrooge, whenever he became thoughtful, to put his hands in his breeches pockets. Pondering on what the Ghost had said, he did so now, but without lifting up his eyes, or getting off his knees.

"You must have been very slow about it, Jacob," Scrooge observed in a businesslike manner, though with humility and deference.

"Slow!" the Ghost repeated.

"Seven years dead," mused Scrooge. "And traveling all the time?"

"The whole time," said the Ghost. "No rest, no peace. Incessant torture of remorse."

"You travel fast?" said Scrooge.

"On the wings of the wind," replied the Ghost.

"You might have got over a great quantity of ground in seven years," said Scrooge.

The Ghost, on hearing this, set up another cry, and clanked its chain so hideously in the dead silence of the night that the Ward would have been justified in indicting it for a nuisance.

"Oh! captive, bound, and double-ironed," cried the phantom, "not to know that ages of incessant labor, by immortal creatures, for this earth must pass into eternity before the good of which it is susceptible is all developed! Not to know that any Christian spirit working kindly in its little sphere, whatever it may be, will find its mortal life too short for its vast means of usefulness! Not to know that no space of regret can make amends for one's life's opportunities misused! Yet such was I! Oh, such was I!"

"But you were always a good man of business, Jacob," faltered Scrooge, who now began to apply this to himself.

"Business!" cried the Ghost, wringing its hands again. "Mankind was my business. The common welfare was my business; charity, mercy, forbearance, and benevolence were, all, my business. The dealings of my trade were but a drop of water in the comprehensive ocean of my business!"

It held up its chain at arm's-length, as if that were the cause of all its unavailing grief, and flung it heavily upon the ground again.

"At this time of the rolling year," the spectre said, "I suffer most. Why did I walk through crowds of fellow-beings with my eyes turned down, and never raise them to that blessed Star which led the Wise Men to a poor abode? Were there no poor homes to which its light would have conducted *me?*"

Scrooge was very much dismayed to hear the spectre going on at this rate, and began to quake exceedingly.

"Hear me!" cried the Ghost. "My time is nearly gone."

"I will," said Scrooge. "But don't be hard upon me! Don't be flowery, Jacob! Pray!"

"How it is that I appear before you in a shape that you can see, I may not tell. I have sat invisible beside you many and many a day."

It was not an agreeable idea. Scrooge shivered, and wiped the perspiration from his brow.

"That is no light part of my penance," pursued the Ghost. "I am here tonight to warn you that you have yet a chance and hope of escaping my fate. A chance and hope of my procuring, Ebenezer."

"You were always a good friend to me," said Scrooge. "Thankee!"

"You will be haunted," resumed the Ghost, "by Three Spirits."

Scrooge's countenance fell almost as low as the Ghost's had done.

"Is that the chance and hope you mentioned, Jacob?" he demanded in a faltering voice.

"It is."

"I—I think I'd rather not," said Scrooge.

"Without their visits," said the Ghost, "you cannot hope to shun the path I tread. Expect the first tomorrow when the bell tolls One."

"Couldn't I take 'em all at once and have it over, Jacob?" hinted Scrooge.

"Expect the second on the next night at the same hour. The third, upon the next night when the last stroke of Twelve has ceased to vibrate. Look to see me no more; and look that, for your own sake, you remember what has passed between us!"

When it had said these words, the spectre took its wrapper from the table, and bound it round its head as before. Scrooge knew this by the smart sound its teeth made when the jaws were brought together by the bandage. He ventured to raise his eyes again, and found his supernatural visitor confronting him in an erect attitude, with its chain wound over and about its arm.

The apparition walked backward from him; and, at every step it took, the window raised itself a little, so that, when the spectre reached it, it was wide open. It beckoned Scrooge to approach, which he did. When they were within two paces of each other, Marley's Ghost held up its hand, warning him to come no nearer. Scrooge stopped.

Not so much in obedience as in surprise and fear; for, on the raising of the hand, he became sensible of confused noises in the air; incoherent sounds of lamentation and regret; wailings inexpressibly sorrowful and self-accusatory. The spectre, after listening for a moment, joined in the mournful dirge; and floated out upon the bleak, dark night.

Scrooge followed to the window, desperate in his curiosity. He looked out.

The air was filled with phantoms, wandering hither and thither in restless haste, and moaning as they went. Every one of them wore chains like Marley's Ghost; some few (they might be guilty governments) were linked together; none was free. Many had been personally known to Scrooge in their lives. He had been quite familiar with one old ghost in a white waistcoat, with a monstrous iron safe attached to its ankle, who cried piteously at being unable to assist a wretched woman with an infant, whom it saw below upon a doorstep. The misery with them all was clearly, that they sought to interfere for good in human matters, and had lost the power for ever.

Whether these creatures faded into mist, or mist enshrouded them, he could not tell. But they and their spirit voices faded together; and the night became as it had been when he walked home.

Scrooge closed the window, and examined the door by which the Ghost had entered. It was double locked, as he had locked it with his own hands, and the bolts were undisturbed. He tried to say "Humbug!" but stopped at the first syllable. And being, from the emotions he had undergone, or the fatigues of the day, or his glimpse of the Invisible World, or the dull conversation of the Ghost, or the lateness of the hour, much in need of repose, went straight to bed without undressing, and fell asleep upon the instant.

MY OWN
TRUE GHOST STORY
by Rudyard Kipling

Impossible to mistake the sound of billiard balls . . .

> *Thirteen*

SOMEWHERE in the Other World, where there are books and pictures and plays and shop-windows to look at, and thousands of men who spend their lives in building up all four, lives a gentleman who writes real stories about the insides of people; and his name is Mr. Walter Besant. But he will insist upon treating his ghosts—he has published half a workshopful of them—with levity. He makes his ghost-seers talk familiarly, and, in some cases, flirt outrageously, with the phantoms. You may treat anything, from a Viceroy to a Vernacular Paper, with levity; but you must behave reverently towards a ghost, and particularly an Indian one.

There are, in this land, ghosts who take the form of fat, cold, pobby corpses, and hide in trees near the roadside till a traveler passes. Then they drop upon his neck and remain. No native ghosts have yet been authentically reported to have frightened an Englishman; but many English ghosts have scared the life out of both white and black.

Nearly every other Station owns a ghost. There are said to be two at Simla, not counting the woman who blows the bellows at Syree dak-bungalow on the Old Road; Mussoorie has a house haunted of a very lively Thing; a White Lady is supposed to do night-watchman round a house at Lahore; Dalhousie says that one of her houses "repeats" on autumn evenings all the incidents of a horrible horse-and-precipice accident; Murree has a merry ghost and, now that she has been swept by cholera, will have room for a sorrowful one; there are Officers' Quarters in Mian Mir whose doors open without reason, and whose furniture is guaranteed to creak, not with the heat of June, but with the weight of Invisibles who come to lounge in the chairs; Peshawar possesses houses that none will willingly rent; there is something—not fever —wrong with a big bungalow in Allahabad. The older Provinces simply bristle with haunted houses, and march phantom armies along their main thoroughfares.

Some of the dak-bungalows on the Grand Trunk Road have handy little cemeteries in their compound—witnesses to the "changes and chances of this mortal life" in the days when men drove from Calcutta to the Northwest. These bungalows are objectionable places to put up in. They are generally very old, always dirty, while the *khansamah* is as ancient as the bungalow. He either chatters senilely, or falls into the long trances of age. In both moods he is useless. If you get angry with him, he refers to some Sahib dead and buried these thirty years, and says that when he was in that Sahib's service not a *khansamah* in the Province could touch him. Then he jabbers and mows and trembles and fidgets among the dishes, and you repent of your irritation.

In these dak-bungalows, ghosts are most likely to be found, and when found, they should be made note of. Not long ago it was my business to live in dak-bungalows. I never inhabited the same house for three nights running, and grew to be learned in the breed. I lived in Government-built ones with red brick walls and rail ceilings, an inventory of the furniture posted in every room, and an excited snake at the threshold to give welcome. I lived in "converted" ones—old houses officiating as dak-bungalows—where nothing was in its proper place, and there wasn't even a fowl for dinner. I lived in second-hand places where the wind blew through open-work marble tracery just as uncomfortably as though it were a broken pane. I lived in dak-bungalows where the last entry in the visitors' book was fifteen months old, and where they slashed off the curry-kid's head with a sword. It was my good luck to meet all sorts of men, from sober traveling missionaries and deserters flying from British Regiments to drunken loafers.

Seeing that a fair proportion of the tragedy of our lives out here acted itself in dak-bungalows, I wondered that I had met no ghosts. A ghost that would voluntarily hang about a dak-bungalow would be mad, of course; but so many men have died mad in dak-bungalows that there must be a fair percentage of lunatic ghosts.

In due time I found my ghost, or ghosts rather, for there were two of them.

We will call the bungalow Katmal dak-bungalow. But *that* was the smallest part of the horror. Katmal dak-bunga-low was old and rotten and unrepaired. The floor was of worn brick, the walls were filthy, and the windows were nearly black with grime. It stood on a bypath largely used by native Sub-Deputy Assistants of all kinds, from Finance to Forest; but real Sahibs were rare. The *khansamah,* who was nearly bent double with old age, said so.

When I arrived, there was a fitful, undecided rain on the face of the land, accompanied by a restless wind, and every gust made a noise like the rattling of dry bones in the stiff toddy-palms outside. The *khansamah* completely lost his head on my arrival. He had served a Sahib once. Did I know that Sahib? He gave me the name of a well-known man who had been buried more than a quarter of a century, and showed me an ancient daguerreotype of that man in his pre-historic youth. I had seen a steel engraving of him at the head of a double volume of memoirs a month before, and I felt ancient beyond telling.

The day shut in and the *khansamah* went to get me food. He did not go through the pretence of calling it "khana"—man's victuals. He said "ratub." That means among other things "grub"—dog's rations. There was no insult in his choice of the term. He had forgotten the other word, I sup-pose.

While he was cutting up the dead bodies of animals, I settled myself down, after exploring the dak-bungalow. There were three rooms, besides my own, which was a corner kennel, each giving into the other through dingy white doors fastened with long iron bars. The bungalow was a very solid one, but the partition walls of the rooms were almost jerry-built in their flimsiness. Every step or bang of a trunk echoed from my room down the other three, and every footfall came back tremulously from the far walls. For this reason I shut the door. There were no lamps—only candles in long glass shades. An oil wick was set in the bathroom.

For bleak, unadulterated misery that dak-bungalow was the worst of the many that I had ever set foot in. There was no fireplace, and the windows would not open; so a brazier of charcoal would have been useless. The rain and wind splashed and gurgled and moaned round the house, and the toddy-palms rattled and roared. Half a dozen jackals went through the compound singing, and a hyena stood afar off and mocked them.

Then came the *ratub*—a curious meal, half native and half English in composition—with the old *khansamah* babbling behind my chair about dead and gone English people, and the wind-blown candles playing shadow-bo-beep with the bed and the mosquito curtains. It was just the sort of dinner and evening to make a man think of every single one of his past sins.

Sleep, for several hundred reasons, was not easy. The lamp in the bathroom threw the most absurd shadows into the room, and the wind was beginning to talk nonsense.

Just when the reasons were drowsy with blood-sucking I heard the regular—"Let-us-take-and-heave-him-over" grunt of doolie-bearers in the compound. First one doolie came in, then a second, and then a third. I heard the doolies dumped on the ground, and the shutter in front of my door shook. "That's some one trying to come in," said I. But no one spoke, and I persuaded myself that it was the gusty wind. The shutter of the room next to mine was attached, and flung back, and the inner door opened. "That's some Sub-Deputy Assistant," I said, "and he has brought his friends with him. Now they'll talk and smoke for an hour."

But there were no voices and no footsteps. No one was putting his luggage into the next room. The door shut, and I thanked Providence that I was to be left in peace. But I was curious to know where the doolies had gone. I got out of bed and looked into the darkness. There was never a sign of a doolie. Just as I was getting into bed again, I heard in the next room the sound that no man in his senses can possibly mistake—the whir of a billiard ball down the length of the slates when the striker is stringing for break. No other sound is like it. A minute afterward there was another whir, and I got into bed. I was not frightened—indeed I was not. I was very curious to know what had become of the doolies. I jumped into bed for that reason.

Next minute I heard the double click of a cannon and my

hair sat up. It is a mistake to say that hair stands up. The
skin of the head tightens and you can feel a faint prickly
bristling all over the scalp, and that is the hair sitting up.

There was a whir and a click, and both sounds could only
have been made by one thing—a billiard ball. I argued the
matter out at great length with myself; and the more I
argued the less probable it seemed that one bed, one table,
and two chairs—all the furniture of the room next to mine
—could so exactly duplicate the sounds of a game of billiards. After another cannon, a three-cushion one to judge
by the whir, I argued no more. I had found my ghost and
would have given worlds to have escaped from that dak-
bungalow. I listened, and with each listen the game grew
clearer. There was a whir on whir and click on click. Sometimes there was a double click and a whir and another click.
Beyond any sort of doubt, people were playing billiards in
the next room. And the room was not big enough to hold a
billiard table.

Between the pauses of the wind I heard the game go forward—stroke after stroke. I tried to believe that I could not
hear voices; but that attempt was a failure.

Do you know what fear is? Not ordinary fear of insult,
injury, or death, but abject, quivering dread of something
that you cannot see—fear that dries the inside of the mouth
and half the throat—fear that makes you sweat on the palms
of the hands, and gulp in order to keep the uvula at work?
This is a fine fear—a great cowardice, and must be felt to
be appreciated. The very improbability of billiards in a dak-

bungalow proved the reality of the thing. No man—drunk or sober—could imagine a game of billiards, or invent the spitting crack of a "screw-cannon."

A severe course of dak-bungalows has this great disadvantage—it breeds infinite credulity. If a man said to a confirmed dak-bungalow haunter, "There's a corpse in the next room, and there's a mad girl in the next but one, and the woman and man on the camel have just eloped from a place sixty miles away," the hearer would not disbelieve because he would know that nothing is too wild, grotesque, or horrible to happen in a dak-bungalow.

This credulity, unfortunately, extends to ghosts. A rational person fresh from his own house would have turned on his side and slept. I did not. So surely as I was given up as a bad carcass by the scores of things in the bed because the bulk of my blood was in my heart, so surely did I hear every stroke of a long game of billiards played in the echoing room behind the iron-barred doors. My dominant fear was that the players might want a marker. It was an absurd fear; because creatures who could play in the dark would be above such superfluities. I only know that this was my terror; and it was real.

After a long while the game stopped, and the door banged. I slept because I was dead tired. Otherwise I should have preferred to have kept awake. Not for everything in Asia would I have dropped the door-bar and peered into the dark of the next room.

When morning came, I considered that I had done well and wisely and inquired for the means of departure.

"By the way, *khansamah,*" said I, "what were those three doolies doing in my compound in the night?"

"There were no doolies," said the *khansamah.*

I went into the next room and the daylight streamed through the open door. I was immensely brave. I would, at that hour, have played Black Pool with the owner of the big Black Pool down below.

"Has this place always been a dak-bungalow?" I asked.

"No," said the *khansamah.* "Ten years or twenty ago, I have forgotten how long, it was a billiard room."

"A how much?"

"A billiard room for the Sahibs who built the railway. I was *khansamah* then in the big house where all the Railway Sahibs lived, and I used to come across with brandy-*shrab.* These three rooms were all one, and they held a big table on which the Sahibs played every evening. But the Sahibs are all dead now, and the railway runs, you say, nearly to Kabul."

"Do you remember anything about the Sahibs?"

"It is long ago, but I remember that one Sahib, a fat man and always angry, was playing here one night, and he said to me, 'Mangal Khan, brandy-*pani* do,' and I filled the glass, and he bent over the table to strike, and his head fell lower and lower till it hit the table, and his spectacles came off, and when we—the Sahibs and myself—ran to lift him, he was dead. I helped to carry him out. Aha, he was a strong Sahib! But he is dead, and I, old Mangal Khan, am still living, by your favor."

That was more than enough! I had my ghost—a first-hand

authenticated article. I would write to the Society for Psychical Research—I would paralyze the Empire with the news! But I would, first of all, put eighty miles of assessed crop-land between myself and that dak-bungalow before nightfall. The Society might send their regular agent to investigate later on.

I went into my own room and prepared to pack after noting down the facts of the case. As I smoked I heard the game begin again—with a miss in balk this time, for the whir was a short one. The door was open and I could see into the room. *Click-click!* That was a cannon. I entered the room without fear, for there was sunlight within and a fresh breeze without. The unseen game was going on at a tremendous rate. And well it might, when a restless little rat was running to and fro inside the dingy ceiling-cloth, and a piece of loose window-sash was making fifty breaks off the window-bolt as it shook in the breeze.

Impossible to mistake the sound of billiard balls! Impossible to mistake the whir of a ball over the slat! But I was to be excused. Even when I shut my enlightened eyes the sound was marvelously like that of a fast game.

Entered angrily the faithful partner of my sorrows, Kadir Baksh.

"This bungalow is very bad and low caste! No wonder the Presence was disturbed and is speckled. Three sets of doolie-bearers came to the bungalow late last night when I was sleeping outside, and said that it was their custom to rest in the rooms set apart for the English people! What honor has the *khansamah?* They tried to enter, but I told them to go. No wonder, if these *Oorias* have been here, that the Presence is sorely sotted. It is shame, and the work of a dirty man."

Kadir Baksh did not say that he had taken from each gang two annas for rent in advance, and then, beyond my earshot, had beaten them with the big green umbrella whose use I could never before divine. But Kadir Baksh has no notions of morality.

There was an interview with the *khansamah,* but as he promptly lost his head, wrath gave way to pity, and pity led to a long conversation, in the course of which he put the fat Engineer-Sahib's tragic death in three separate stations—two of them fifty miles away. The third shift was to Calcutta, and there the Sahib died while driving a dog-cart.

If I had encouraged him, the *khansamah* would have wandered all through Bengal with his corpse.

I did not go away as soon as I intended. I stayed for the night, while the wind and the rat and the sash and the window-bolt played a ding-dong "hundred and fifty up." Then the wind ran out and the game of billiards stopped, and I felt that I had ruined my one, genuine, hall-marked ghost story.

Had I only stopped at the proper time, I could have made *anything* out of it. That was the bitterest thought of all!

Elizabeth Hough Sechrist

became interested in writing for children while she was a Children's Librarian in Bethlehem, Pennsylvania. Each year she was asked by boys and girls, teachers and librarians, for information on Christmas in other lands. Because of the lack of material, she began to collect and write on the subject herself, and the resulting book, CHRISTMAS EVERYWHERE, has been popular in schools and libraries for many years.

After nine years' experience in Bethlehem and Pittsburgh libraries, Mrs. Sechrist gave up her work to devote her time to writing, editing, and lecturing on children's books—and, incidentally, to keeping house. She and her husband live in York, Pennsylvania.